TRAIL MIX 1: AMOEBA

TRAIL MIX 1: AMOEBA

BY

PIERS ANTHONY

TRAIL MIX 1: AMOEBA

eISBN: 978-0-9832929-7-5
Print ISBN: 978-1-62467-205-7

PREMIER
DIGITAL PUBLISHING

Published by Premier Digital Publishing
www.premierdigitalpublishing.com
Follow us on Twitter @PDigitalPub
Follow us on Facebook: Premier Digital Publishing

This is a work of fiction. Names, characters, places, and incidents either are the product of the author's imagination or are used fictitiously. Any resemblance to actual persons, living or dead, events, or locales is entirely coincidental.

CHAPTER 1: TRAIL

Tod Timmins paused, blinking. Of course he hadn't just seen an odd trail leading away from the warehouse. This was the city; there were streets here, not trails. He marched on into the warehouse, ready for his day of manual labor.

But it bothered him. His job was dull, good for the body, but a waste of mind. He would like something more intellectually challenging, but in this day a man was lucky to have a job, any job, that paid his way. He simply could not afford to be choosy. Maybe if he had a loyal wife at home, or a lovely rich girlfriend, he would be more satisfied. But as it was, his job was virtually the whole of his life, and it wasn't enough.

Well, he did have his private vice. When alone he would take out his little polished wooden ocarina and tootle on it. It was a kind of closed recorder with eight finger holes on top and two thumb holes on the bottom, and played mellow notes. Over the years he had become reasonably skilled with it, though he was no musician, and could play any melody he heard by ear. This gave him pleasure, easing his boredom and tension. But neither was this enough, in itself; it merely diverted him from the deadly overall dullness of his existence. He wished there could be just one person he could play for who would truly appreciate it. But he had never dared even inquire, fearing ridicule. A man who could heave heavy crates around, tootling on what looked like a toy whistle?

So when he saw the path again, this time leading from the corner of the parking lot, Tod shrugged and followed it. What the hell; maybe it simply led to the next warehouse, satisfying his errant curiosity.

It did not. It wound through the city, along a street without actually intersecting it; Tod saw cars crossing it without quite being there. It was as if this were an overhead bypass, though it was at ground level. He began to feel dizzy trying to get the perspective right, and decided to leave that for another time. He focused on the trail, and the cars seemed to fade out, replaced by vegetation. This was one unusual experience.

Suddenly he was in a forest. He stopped, looking back. Had he been walking through a park and not noticing? Maybe he had been thinking instead of observing, but this was strange. He had never before been this absent-minded.

He walked back the way he had come. The forest faded and the street appeared, along with the local vegetation. There was no transition; it just happened, like a scene shift in a movie. How could this be?

Tod stepped back and forth several times, verifying it. Forward one step put him in the forest; backward returned him to the city. The trail continued forward, but ended backward, where he had taken it. Weird!

Curious, he experimented. He found the exact spot the change occurred, and moved his head with clock-like slowness, watching. Now he saw that the change was gradual, the trail proceeding through the city, out to the country, and into the forest. All at accelerated speed, so that when he walked normally it was as if he were racing at a hundred miles an hour or faster, condensing the shift. The trail itself did not race, merely the cityscape beyond it, in an enhanced perspective, as if it were a projected background picture being rapidly scanned. Fascinating!

So this was definitely not a natural path. It was something supernatural, appearing where it should not be, and operating in a revved-up manner. It seemed to be no accident that he had found it, but rather an offering. *Here am I, your special trail; take me*.

Did he want to? Tod was bored with his life, but not foolish. He had no idea where the trail led. Did he really want to risk it? It could be dangerous, luring him in and conveying him to some soul-eating monster. Or to some marvelous fantasy fairyland where his fondest dreams would come true. It was surely a considerable gamble, either way. He would have to think about this.

Well, no time like the present. He stood there and brought out his ocarina. Music loosened his mind, enabling him to perceive alternative perspectives. He played a simple melody, serenading the limited landscape. Would his music make it fade?

It did not. The outline of the path seemed to intensify, and the foliage brightened, seeming almost to orient the leaves to better receive the tune. Maybe he was just imagining it, but this seemed like genuine appreciation. This trail liked his playing!

Or more likely he was so eager for applause that his eye conjured reactions that were not there. That way lay insanity. He put away the ocarina.

He walked back to the parking lot and off the end of the trail. He had no trouble doing this, despite a certain background apprehension. Some situations were easier to get into than out of. It seemed that this was entirely voluntary.

Tod drove home. And there was the trail, leading up to his house. It was definitely courting him.

He pondered for an hour before recognizing that he was hooked. The trail was a puzzle: where did it lead? Why was it offering itself to him? Did it really like his simple music? Tod was good at puzzles, and did them constantly in his off hours. There were hardly any he did not eventually solve. He would be unable to rest until he solved this one. He also liked nature, and that forest was nature. The way the trail changed, there was surely something else beyond the forest. He wanted to see it. He could not be sure how long it would wait for him; if he delayed too long, it might fade out and his chance would be forever lost.

The weekend was coming up. He packed a knapsack with supplies, then dug out his hiking clothing, compass, and walking staff. He was ready for a two day camp-out. That should at least satisfy his curiosity, and at most—who knew what he might find?

He got a good night's sleep, ate a good breakfast, closed the house, and set off down the trail. He was exhilarated; for good or for ill, he had made this much of a commitment.

In a moment he was in the low foliage with the street becoming unreal, then the forest. Soon he saw that the landscape was changing further; the trees were becoming larger, and their colors were changing. Not in the manner of fall, but more like an alien terrain. Some of the trunks were green, some blue, and the leaves ranged from black and white to rainbow hues. This was no longer anything local.

Yet the air was good, and the gravity normal, and the temperature was perfect for light exercise. He liked this environment very well so far.

Still, there had to be a kicker. What was it?

He came to a stream that crossed the trail. It came from somewhere in the forest, and returned there, with some moss on its banks and small fish darting around. There was no bridge, so he took off his hiking boots and socks and waded through it. The water was cold but not uncomfortably so. He paused to scoop out a handful and taste it: clear and potable. No pollution. This was definitely a pristine realm.

The forest disappeared, replaced by rolling hills covered with brightly colored plants: red, green, blue, yellow, white, black. Many of them bore berries or fruits. They looked tempting, but Tod was cautious.

Then he came to a shape on the trail. He gripped his staff firmly; it could be used for self-defense if necessary. That was part of its purpose, though normally intended to dissuade poisonous snakes or poke suspicious mounds.

It turned out to be a woman, garbed in a brown smock. She was hunched over, trying to heave her guts out. Vomit was spattered across the trail and on her smock.

Tod was not sure what to do. Obviously she was no threat to him, unless she had a contagious disease. More likely she had eaten something that made her sick. How could he help her?

"Hello," he said, sounding a bit inane in his own ears. He wasn't sure she spoke his language; she did not look like a local woman. Her skin was swarthy as if she haled from the tropics, and her proportions seemed odd, though that could be the clothing.

She heard him and glanced up. "Go away." Then, after a pause, "Please."

"I just want to help, if I can."

"Make me unsick!" she flared.

Tod almost smiled. "I'll try. What did you eat?"

She made a couple of dry heaves, then lifted her upper body and pointed. "Blue berries. I thought they—" She paused to heave again. "Were good. I ate many."

So the appealing blue berries were poisonous. "Maybe water, to clear them out of your stomach. I have some." He brought out his canteen and proffered it.

She just looked at it. "A rock?"

Oh. Definitely not from his culture. "A canteen." He unscrewed the cap, then tilted it to pour a few drops of water. He brought it to his mouth and drank a sip, demonstrating. Then he wiped it off and proffered it again. "Water."

"Water," she repeated. She took the canteen and sipped from it as he had done.

"More. Drink enough so it dilutes the poison and you can puke it out."

"Ah." She drank more deeply. Then in a moment she heaved once more, expelling bluish water.

"Again," he said. "Get it clear."

She drank again, vomited again, but looked more comfortable. "Thank you," she said, returning the canteen to him. "I feel less worse."

"You're welcome." He was relieved that it had worked. "I am Tod Timmins, of America."

She remained kneeling on the ground. "I am Veee."

"Venus?"

"Veee."

"Vee."

"Veee," she said firmly, extending the vowel sound.

"Veee," he agreed, getting it at last. He had never heard of such a name, but it only confirmed she was from another culture.

"I will try to stand now."

"May I help you?"

"Yes, of course." She took his proffered arm and hauled herself to her feet. She was a solid woman, not fat but far from lean, almost as tall as he was, with a mat of brown hair to her waist. Her smock was more than spattered with vomit; in fact it was soaked in front.

Tod stepped back. "Are you all right now?"

Veee took a step, wavered, caught herself, and stood unsteadily. "No." Then she heaved out more water.

"You had better sit down, or lie down for a while," Tod said. "Until you recover."

"Yes." But she didn't move.

"What is it?"

"I am—weakening."

"Can you walk?"

"No. I will fall."

"You need to get cleaned up."

She glanced at herself. "Yes."

"There's a stream not far back. You could rinse your clothing."

"Yes. I will do it when I get the strength."

"Or I could do it for you."

"Do what?" she asked with seeming resignation.

What did she think? "Rinse your smock. Fetch more water."

"Oh. Yes. I am not normally so helpless. This illness embarrasses me. I will let you do it." She started to remove her smock.

Tod turned away.

"Why do you avert your gaze?" Veee asked.

"To spare you further embarrassment from exposure."

"You are not like the men I have known."

"Thank you, I think. In my land, women do not go naked, and do not like to have strange men see them that way."

"In my land, we have no choice." That might explain something: she thought a man would routinely take advantage of an ill woman. "Here is my garment."

Tod put his hand back and took it. Then he thought of something else. "Are you cold?"

"Yes."

What could he do? He removed knapsack and set it aside. Then his hiking jacket, and his shirt. "Put these on," he said, handing them back.

There was a rustle as she worked with what was evidently unfamiliar clothing. "They do not cover my legs."

Tod removed his heavy hiking boots, and trousers and handed the last back too. Now he stood in trunks and T-shirt. He put his boots back on.

"You are a handsome man," Veee remarked, evidently appreciating his backside.

Tod found himself flattered. He did not regard himself as handsome, but he did have his heavy-lifting muscles and was in reasonable shape. "Thank you. I will wash your clothing now." He walked away without looking at her, uncertain how well she was covered.

He followed the curving trail through the brush to the stream and rinsed her smock as well as he could. It seemed to be made from some kind of animal hide, light but strong. The blue vomit stains washed right out.

He wrung it as dry as he could, then carried it back to where Veee sat, along with his refilled canteen. She now wore his shirt, jacket, and trousers and looked relatively western. Her breasts and hips strained against clothing that was made for a man. But she did not look well. She was pale and hunched over. Even her luxuriant hair looked tangled.

"How are you doing?" he asked her.

"Your apparel helps, but I remain weak and cold. I fear my illness has not yet run its course."

Tod made a decision. "My home is not far away. Let me carry you there. Then you can rest, and I'll call a doctor."

"Yes, if you wish." Again that assumption that the man's will governed.

He approached her, handed her her damp smock, then put his forearms behind her back and knees, and heaved her up. She was less solid than he had feared, weighing perhaps a hundred and fifty pounds, and she cooperated by putting an arm around his neck. He was accustomed to toting heavy boxes, and could handle this.

He tramped along the trail. Soon the scenery changed, becoming the forest, and then his yard and house. Veee's eyes widened in evident amazement, but she did not speak. He carried her to the door, set her carefully on her feet, dug out his key from the pocket of the pants she wore, opened the door, then carried her inside. Like a marriage, he thought, taking his bride across the threshold. But this was far from that.

He laid her down on his living room couch. She was shivering; she must be starting to run a fever. The poison remaining in her system was still running its course, as she had surmised.

He fetched a thick blanket and was about to put it over her, but she shook her head no, not trusting it. He set it still folded on the armrest beyond her feet. Meanwhile her shivering only worsened. "I'm worried about you," he said. "Let me call a neighbor. She's a nurse, and will know better than I do what you need."

She looked at him, surprised, then spoke a stream of sheer

gibberish. It was evidently a language, but like none he had heard before.

"I don't understand you," he said. "Why the change?"

She spoke again, seeming as perplexed as he was. Then she looked at the door.

This he understood. "The trail! We understood each other on the trail, but now it's all Greek!"

She nodded agreement, responding to his tone. They were indeed of different cultures, and somehow the trail had made them understand each other. Probably she had been speaking her language all the time, and he had heard it as his own, and vice versa for her.

Still, she needed help. He picked up the phone and called the neighbor. "Meg, Tod here, I have a situation, a woman needs help. Can you come over?"

She had known him since he was a child, and had sometimes babysat him. "Sure Tod."

Belatedly he realized he remained in T-shirt, undershorts, and boots. He hastily dug out and donned new shirt and pants. His wallet remained in the pants Veee wore.

Soon she arrived, a heavyset older woman who exuded competence in her specialty. Tod showed her to the living room, where Veee lay shivering on the couch.

"Where is the woman?" Meg asked.

"Right there." He gestured to the couch.

"Where?"

Was she suddenly blind? "Right here," he said, resting a hand on Veee's shivering shoulder.

"Mr. Timmins, I have not thought of you as a jokester. That is an empty couch except for a blanket." Her use of his formal name was significant; she was annoyed.

"You really can't see her?" he asked incredulously.

"Are you on medication?"

Tod smiled. "You think I'm hallucinating?"

"You tell me: do you really think there is a woman on that couch?"

Something truly strange was happening here. "Yes. I found her outside, sick and shivering. I brought her in and called you to try to help her. I don't know why you can't see her. Here, maybe if you touch her hand." He lifted Veee's hand. "Here."

Meg came and touched where Tod held up the hand. Her hand passed through it and came up against his own hand below.

Tod stared, stunned. So did Veee. *She had no substance here!* Not for anyone except Tod. She was in effect a ghost.

"Satisfied?" Meg inquired gently.

"I—I guess I saw a ghost," Tod said. "Maybe I haven't gotten enough sleep. I—I'm sorry to have bothered you for nothing, Meg."

She nodded grimly. "Whatever your new meds are, get off them," she said, and departed.

He was not on any meds, but could hardly blame her. He was having enough trouble grasping what he had seen, and appreciated her skepticism.

Tod proffered the blanket again, and this time Veee accepted it. He laid it carefully on her—and watched it sink through her body, clothing and all, and come to rest on the couch. Veee was real only to Tod. Maybe she had some fractional substance, like fog, so that she didn't sink through the couch, but she could not support anything above her.

But she was wearing his clothing. How could that be ghostly?

The question brought the likely answer: she had donned the clothing on the trail. Now it associated with her, and shared her attributes. Probably if he put it back on, while on the trail, it would resume association with him and return to reality in his world. More was happening on the trail than what was immediately apparent.

"Veee, I'm sorry," Tod said. "You can't be in my realm."

She nodded agreement, reacting to his tone and what they both had seen.

"I'll take you back to the trail. I'll help you there." He reached below her and picked her up. Now he realized that she was lighter than she had been, and her body barely dented the couch.

He carried her out the door. Then he thought of something. "If you don't mind, I'd like to try just one more thing."

She nodded again, amenable to whatever he had in mind. He carried her around the house, into the alley.

She became ghostlike, then faded entirely. Hastily he backtracked, and she reappeared, gaining weight. She existed here only in the ambiance of the trail, which must partly infuse his house, but did not extend beyond it. They were both creatures of the trail, in their fashion, able to interact with each other, but not with anyone else. Not in this world.

He marched on to the trail, took a few more steps to be certain, then set her down, keeping his hands on her to be sure she was steady. She was now reassuringly solid, though still shivering. It was not cold here, but she clearly was suffering. She did not seem to be running a fever, but her body must be making the effort. "I'll be right back," he said.

"I'll wait," she agreed.

"We're speaking to each other again!" he exclaimed.

"Yes!"

He enfolded her and kissed her on the mouth. She met his lips firmly, with no pretense of shyness or reluctance. Then almost immediately he withdrew. "I'm sorry. I didn't mean to do that. I just—

the relief—"

"You desire me," she said.

"No! I mean, not that way. I just—"

"I understand. I kissed you back. We're both relieved."

"Yes. Now I'll fetch some stuff to get you warm, here."

"Thank you."

Tod returned to his house, picked up the blanket, then rummaged to find a small one-person tent he used for camping. He brought both out to the trail. He wrapped the blanket around Veee, noting that now it did relate to her, then went to work setting up the tent. He had her crawl into it and lie wrapped in the blanket.

Still she shivered. More was needed. Could he light a fire? He doubted that was wise; the city was visible beyond the edge of the trail, and he couldn't be sure the blaze would be invisible.

"I can bring out more blankets," he said.

"Please, warm me," she said.

"I'm trying to!"

"In my country we share warmth, when we need to."

"Body warmth," he agreed. "But you're a woman."

"I will give you what you want, for the warmth." Her lips were blue. She was desperate.

"All I want is to help you," he said. Then he stripped back down to his trunks and got into the tent with her. She opened her jacket and shirt, and drew off her trousers. She had remarkably healthy limbs.

He clasped her closely, their two nearly bare bodies pressed together from neck to knees. They managed to wrap the two of them up snugly in the blanket.

"Thank you," she breathed.

Now he became aware of several things. She was indeed cold, not feverish; her body felt as if she had just emerged from a chill swim. She was well endowed, better than he had first thought, with large breasts pressing against his chest and solid thighs against his legs. She was muscular, yes, but also lean elsewhere; there was no flab on her, and her waist and neck were small.

All of which had an effect on his mindless body. He was getting an erection. It swelled urgently between them, impossible for her to miss.

"I will give you," she repeated, understanding.

"No. I'm a man; I can't help reacting. But I am trying to warm you, not seduce you."

"Don't seduce me; just take me."

"I wouldn't do that!"

"Why not?"

"It—it is more of a commitment than I wish to give. When a man has sex with a woman, he is generally thinking of marrying her, or at least a serious relationship. Not always, not with some men, but with me, yes. I hardly know you; our association is sheer coincidence. I would not force casual sex on you."

"In my land, a man takes a woman when he wants her. What she wants does not matter. In any event, it is soon over, and he leaves her alone until the urge comes on him again."

"In my land, we call that rape."

She paused. "I think I grasp your term, thanks to this unusual compatibility of language we have here on the trail, but it does not exist in my land. A woman has no power to refuse, so cannot be forced. If she does not wish it, she must avoid the man, if she can, or associate with a stronger man who will reserve her to himself. I have had no protector; I have been taken many times. Sometimes I liked it. Always I pretended pleasure, so I would not get beaten."

Tod suffered a small revelation. "Is that why you left your land?"

She smiled against his cheek. "In part. There was also my shame.

Mostly, I was curious where the path led."

Her shame? He decided not to inquire about that, yet. "Me too."

"We are kindred, in that respect."

"So it seems," he agreed.

"You seem to be a nice man." The way she said it made it seem like an extreme rarity. Her culture must be a rough one.

"I try to be."

"I am warming." Indeed, her torso felt less cold. "Now that you know me better, do you wish it? It is not of special value to me, and it will not demean me if you take it. I am long past that."

Tod was tempted. His erection remained uncomfortably hard. She was not his idea of the perfect pinup, but his proximity to her solidly female torso made his body get ideas regardless of his preference. It had been some time since he had been intimate with a woman. If she truly didn't mind...Still did not seem right. "If it is not something you want, then I don't want it either." Though his stiff penis was giving away the lie.

"You are warm. Your warmth inside me would heat me better."

What a rationale! "But do you want it?"

"I want to please you, so you will keep me warm."

"That was not my question."

"I have not been asked that question before. I must consider an answer."

Tod had an idea. "While you do, do you mind if I play my music?" Because this might help take his mind off his member, and enable him to be more objective about this whole situation.

"Music?"

He fumbled in the pocket of his pants where they lay beside the tent and fetched the ocarina. He brought it to his mouth, separated his hands from her body, and played the simplest of melodies.

Her whole body stiffened against him.

Tod stopped. "I'm sorry. I did not mean to upset you."

She relaxed. "I am amazed, not upset. I think that is the loveliest sound I have ever heard. I could not believe it came from you."

Oh. She had not encountered this kind of musical instrument before. "It's an ocarina. A small closed woodwind. I blow in it, and cover the holes, and make the notes. Do you wish to try it?"

"You will allow me to touch it? In my village, only the shaman plays the whistle, and he is not nearly as good as you."

"You may touch it," he said. "In my world we have many such instruments. They are not remarkable or magic."

"Yes, I will." She threaded her arms up so she could take the instrument. She blew into the mouthpiece. A thin erratic whistle sounded. "Oh, it doesn't like me!"

"Like this," Tod said. He set her hands on it more properly, fingers firmly over the holes, his own fingers over hers to guide them. "Now blow."

She did. This time there was a steady note. "Oh!" she repeated, this time delighted.

"Now lift only your smallest right finger."

She did, and blew. A slightly higher note sounded.

"Now lift also your second smallest finger on the right hand."

She did. Another note sounded. Soon he had her playing a mini scale up and down. She was an apt learner, especially considering that she had never encountered such an instrument before.

She returned the ocarina to him, and he returned it to his trouser pocket. Then she put her arms about him and kissed him almost savagely. "I nearly want it."

But it would be taking advantage of her in her excitement. "When you are sure. Not before."

"You are unlike any man I have known."

"Thank you, I think. Maybe now we can sleep. There's not much else to do." He found he did not mind being pressed so close to her, apart from the awkwardness of his reaction; she was comfortable physically, and to an increasing extent, mentally and emotionally. She knew he was sexually excited, and was comfortable with it and ready to accommodate it whenever the time was right; that made a considerable difference.

"Yes."

He sighed. "We live in interesting times."

"I do not understand."

"It's a saying we have. Actually it's a curse, because interesting times are generally times of upheaval, famine, and war. It's better to live in dull times."

"Maybe. My times are dull, but I think I prefer your interesting ones."

"Even being pressed against a man whose hunger for your body is manifest, but who won't indulge it?"

"Yes," she repeated seriously.

They relaxed, still pressed together, and to his surprise Tod did sleep. He dreamed, of course, of sex.

He woke in the night, relieved in a way that night existed here on the trail. He needed to urinate.

He started to unwrap himself. That woke Veee. "You are going?"

"I must pee."

She chuckled. "So must I. My gut is empty, but I did drink water."

"Let's do it, then return to our sleep."

"Yes."

They got free of the blanket and the tent. The sky was bright with stars, but the familiar constellations were not there. "Do you want privacy?" he asked her.

"I am warming, but I remain weak. Please hold me in place."

They moved into the brush. The light was dim, but it was possible to see their way. She found a suitable spot and squatted, and he put his hands on her shoulders to hold her steady. He heard the rush of her urine striking the ground. Then she stood, and he faced a bush and tried to urinate, but his penis remained somewhat thickened and it was difficult. Finally he managed to get it started, and then it flowed, albeit somewhat thinly.

They returned to the tent and embraced, face to face, as before. "I will give you," she said again.

"Do you want it?" he asked again.

"I have pondered, and concluded that I can't answer that question."

"Why not? It's an answer I need to have."

"Because if I tell you I do not want it, then when you want it, it will be difficult for me to pretend. So I can't tell you that."

"I think you have answered me, though. You don't want it."

"I did not say that."

"Of course. But it's true."

"I think I must give you a larger part of an answer. You are a decent man, and I want to please you, and to that extent I want it. But I will like it better if I come to want it for myself alone, as I think you want me to, and I am not there yet. I am capable of liking it when I like the man. As you said, we are relative strangers to each other."

"That's a good answer."

"It is difficult, because I know you do desire me, and I want so much to make you happy." His turgid member against her belly could hardly be mistaken. "Would you settle for a kiss?"

"Yes!" Because he was coming to like her, apart from the sexual passion, and that was part of the way he wanted her.

They squeezed each other and kissed. She melted into him, and his liking for her increased.

"It is so close," she murmured. "Are you sure—?"

"I am sure it is not yet time," he said regretfully.

They kissed again, and settled down for the rest of the night. And of course Tod couldn't sleep, and not just because of his erection. There were so many mysteries here!

"I have disturbed you," Veee said. "I should have found a better answer."

"Your answer was fine. What you want is love."

"Love?" It seemed that concept was new to her.

Tod explained it as well as he could: that passion man and woman felt for each other that went well beyond sex. "So you see, I have had sex with women, but never love. Some of those women were paid; they were whores. It is true romantic love I crave. For a woman to truly desire me. If you wanted me that way, then I'd love to have sex with you."

"I know men can love women, but I know of no women loving a man. Not the way you describe. She only accommodates him."

"Maybe you can be the first to love, some day," he said, laughing.

"Is love like this?" She kissed him lingeringly. There was a new quality to it.

"Yes," he agreed as he recovered. "Only because you truly feel that way, not because you are acting."

"Maybe some day I will not need to act."

"Some day," he agreed. Then, still conscious of his hard member pressing against her, he fell asleep.

In the morning they got up and shared the staples he had in his pack. They were strange to Veee, but she ate them with increasing relish. "My gut is better now," she said. "My strength is recovering, thanks to you."

"Thanks to my body warmth," he agreed.

"Thanks to your understanding and caring. And your music. I have not before encountered that in a man."

Tod laughed. "Welcome to it, Veee."

Her smock was not yet dry, so she dressed again in his clothing. "You are very kind to lend me this," she said. "I have no way to repay you in kind. Maybe I should—"

"No," he said gently.

Impulsively, she kissed him again. "I think it will not be long before I truly want it."

"I look forward to that," he said gallantly.

"Now that I am mending, we must decide: should we return to our own realms, as we can not share each other's realms?"

Tod considered. Veee's problem had diverted him from his exploration of the trail. "I want to see where the trail goes. I am curious by nature. And—I must be honest here—I have some hope that in time you will—want it. You are the only woman who has expressed any real interest in me, and I—I value that."

"I want to see the trail's end too. You are the only man who has given me a choice. Who has seen me as a person. I hope too that soon I will want it in the way you wish, so that you will have no further reticence."

"But you have to understand that since we can't go into each other's worlds, we can have no permanent association. Whatever we feel and do is only on the trail."

She nodded. "We are temporary friends."

"Possibly temporary lovers."

She was quick to agree. "Temporary lovers."

"Then I think we are agreed," he said, relieved. "We travel on."

"We are agreed," she agreed.

CHAPTER 2: BEM

Tod returned to his house to amend his knapsack supplies. He added a folding canvas bucket, and several cans of fire mix in case they had to cook, together with lighters. Then, as an afterthought, a pistol and ammunition, for hunting or defense. His food was limited, and they did not care to risk more poisonous berries. It was mostly chance that Tod had not sampled any himself. So he shared his trail mix with Veee, and she was hungry and had no trouble with it. He did not mention the gun to her, not because of any distrust of her, but because he doubted she would understand, or like it if she did. Women could be extremely wary of guns.

"But you know," he said as they moved out. "My food will not last long. We need to be able to forage from the trail." He had started slow, in case her weakness remained, but she seemed to have recovered and had no trouble matching his pace.

"Yes. Otherwise we can't stay long."

"It doesn't make sense to me that the trail should seek us out, then try to poison us. There must be some misunderstanding."

"I had not thought of that," she said. "There must be good berries and bad berries. I thought the blue ones were good. They tasted good."

Tod paused, looking at the berries. "Would it bother you if I tried some, carefully?"

"Not the blue ones!"

"Not the blue ones," he agreed, with a faint shudder. "How about the red ones?"

"Let me taste first. I think I will know soon if they will sicken me. I learn quickly about poisons."

That made sense. "But carefully. Very carefully."

She picked a single red berry and barely touched it to her teeth, evoking a spot of red juice. She savored that. "I think it is good."

"I'll try it, then."

She stayed his hand. "Not yet. It takes a bit for the effect to start. I had time to eat many before I felt it." She chewed and swallowed the berry.

They waited apprehensively for the reaction, but none came. She ate another berry, then a third.

Tod was satisfied. "I think it's safe."

"Not yet," she said. "Let me wait the time it took for me to sicken before. Then we will be sure."

That made sense. They waited.

To pass the time, Tod brought out his ocarina. "My I play?"

"Oh, do!" she agreed rapturously.

This time he played fancier melodies, enjoying them. Veee watched and listened, smiling. She truly appreciated the music, and that was a fulfillment of Tod's secret dream: to have someone care about his art. The trail was fulfilling more of his ambition, in quiet ways.

The time came, and she remained well. "It is safe." She fell to and began eating red berries rapidly.

Tod ate also, but more cautiously. He ate one red berry, and it was juicy and delicious. He ate another, savoring it similarly. He ate a third.

"Stop there," Veee recommended. "Just in case."

He obeyed. He played more melodies on his ocarina, basking in the adoration of the music that Veee evinced. He knew she wasn't pretending; it was transporting her. That pleased him; he appreciated her appreciation.

Then she surprised him. "Music is an art. You are an artist."

"Oh, I just play what I like," he protested. "I'm no musician. I don't compare to the real musicians we have."

"I am an artist too. It is my shame."

He thought he had misheard. "Your what?"

"I made a sand picture, with colored sands," Veee said. "Knowing it was not allowed. Only men can be artists. But I simply had to express myself. I was alone; I did not know anyone was watching. I meant to erase it before I left, so no one would know. But a man was suspicious, and he hid himself near that sand place, and watched until I came. So they caught me. They banished me from the village for a week. I knew if I ever did it again, they would cut off my hands and leave me to die. So I did not do it again. But after that, no man would marry me. They tolerated me, they spouted their hard penises into me, but I knew I had to leave."

"Oh, Veee! That is horrible!"

"Yes, I should never have made that sand painting. I have been ashamed ever since. But I had to tell you, before you came to like me any better."

"I meant what they did to you! Punishing you like that for expressing yourself."

She glanced sidelong at him with no trace of coquetry. "You can forgive me that?"

"Forgive you! Veee, in my world we are proud to have artists, male and female. You were never at fault."

Still she was cautious. "You are not repelled?"

"Veee, no, never! Please, make a sand painting for me. I want to see it."

She nodded as if being asked to do something repulsive. Then she cleared a place on the trail, fetched handfuls of sand, and made a flower pattern. There were only two shades of sand available, so it was in effect monochrome, but it was lovely and realistic regardless.

"Veee, it's beautiful. I want to kiss you."

"If you kiss me, I will know whether you mean it."

"You sure will," he agreed. He embraced her and kissed her passionately.

She melted against him. "You do mean it," she breathed.

"Oh, yes. Veee, we are similar, again: my music, your painting. Guilty secrets that don't have to be secret any more."

"Yes," she agreed gladly. "Oh, Tod, I think I am ready to give you what you want."

"Maybe it's time," he agreed, as gladly.

And felt the first tinge of queasiness. "Uh-oh."

"But it's safe!" Veee protested. "I have no sickness."

"Maybe for you. But me—" He lurched away, leaned over, and puked out a red stream.

"How can this be?" Veee asked plaintively. "I tested them."

Todd continued heaving until his gut was satisfied that nothing worth puking remained. He drank from his canteen and vomited again. Then a surge of weakness came, and he sat down.

"I am so sorry!" she said, putting a hand on his shoulder. "I thought it was safe."

"At least I didn't eat much."

"The weakness is upon you. Then comes the shivering. Then health returns. You are weak sooner than I was, so you should get better more quickly."

"That is reassuring to know." Already he was experiencing the first chill.

"I will warm you."

"There is no need."

But there was a need, and it was evident. He was starting to shiver violently. It was the heat of day, but he was in sudden misery.

Veee efficiently unpacked and set up the tent and put the blanket in. She had learned very quickly. She was from a primitive culture, but was clearly quite smart.

She helped him crawl into the tent. She worked off his shirt and trousers. Then she doffed her own, got in next to him, and wrapped them both in the blanket. Her body was soft and hot, and a great comfort as its heat spread to him.

"No hardness," she murmured, smiling.

He realized it was true: he had no erection. He was simply too miserable for that.

"Are you sure it wasn't my confession of shame that sickened you?"

"Veee—" Then he realized she was teasing him. She now had the confidence to do that.

She held him close, and gradually his coldness eased. He slept, warmed and comforted by her embrace.

He wasn't sure how much time passed before he woke. She was immediately aware of it. "You are better."

She was right, but he wondered how she knew so soon.

"Hard," she said. Now he understood: He had his erection back. He had to laugh. But his lingering weakness vitiated any real desire he might have had for sex. He might have an erection, but he knew he would not be able to climax.

"Thanks for taking care of me," he said.

"I did what you did, desiring you in your closeness."

"But you never got hard."

"I got soft," she said. They laughed together.

It turned out that he had slept less than an hour, by his watch. He had recovered much faster than Veee had. That made sense, because he had eaten much less, and far more slowly. Still the mystery remained: "Why did I get sick, when you didn't?"

She considered. "The colors. Maybe blue makes me sick, and red makes you sick."

"Gender related? That's odd."

"Try a blue one. A little."

His appetite was returning. He picked a blue berry and at it with extreme caution. He had no reaction, even after time passed. He ate another. He did not get sick. "Apparently that's it. Men can eat the blue ones, women the red ones. Now we know."

"We will stay with our own kind."

Could it really be that simple? Yet they had the evidence of the sickness—and non-sickness.

Tod's normal vigor came back. He was ready to travel again.

They walked on along the trail. "You have seen my residence," Tod said. "Where is yours?"

"Down the side trail. I got sick at the intersection."

"I mean where geographically? In what section of the world?"

"Our legends tell of a great warm land we left, and of boats across water, and a great new land, but colder. That is all I know."

"You have no maps?"

"Hunting maps, to track the prey? Only men can see them."

"Do you have any written histories?"

"Written?" she asked blankly. "Histories?"

Evidently not. Her society was primitive. He was surprised that it still existed; he thought all the obscure corners of the Earth had been explored. He decided to let it go.

The trail wound around low hills, then reached larger ones, and finally mountains. They followed it as it became a ledge in the slope of a snow-covered peak, awesomely high above the valley.

There at another intersection stood a form. It resembled a child's humorous statue, being blob-shaped and candy striped. What was it doing here?

They approached it and paused. Had it somehow been brought up the other trail? That trail led steeply down into the obscurity below. Why had it been left here?

The statue whistled from a vent just below a knob that might be its head. "Greeting, alien travelers."

It spoke! Or whistled, and Tod understood the meaning.

"Greeting, creature," Tod said, surprised. It seemed Veee deferred to him, honoring her female place, so had not spoken.

"I am Beobrumemmik, of Snalliverti," the creature said, a faint band of color traversing its knob.

That was too much for Tod to assimilate. "May I simply call you Bem? This is generic for—never mind."

"As you wish."

"I am Tod, and this is Veee. We are traveling together, exploring this mysterious trail."

"And my greeting to you, Veee," Bem said, more color showing around the knob. That might be a smile. Evidently it could see and hear them, maybe via the knob.

"Hello, Bem."

"Are the two of you of a multi-gendered species? I inquire not to give offense, but to clarify, noting minor distinctions in your forms. My own species is single-gendered."

Tod and Veee exchanged a glance. "Yes, we are human beings, of male and female genders. So you are asexual?"

"I am, as the more efficient species generally are, again no offense intended."

"None taken," Tod said, smiling. "How did you come here?"

"I spied a trail. I am of an inquisitive disposition, so I followed it. It led here. I am uncertain which fork to take, so I wait for illumination."

"We come from our homes at the ends of this branch, and it seems that no other creature on the trail can share our homes," Tod said. "So we are exploring forward, as it were. You are welcome to join us, if you wish. We ask only that you not seek to harm us, and we will not seek to harm you."

"This is reassuring, and I agree. Your forms are quite alien to me, though humanoid animals do exist in my frame, but your speech is familiar."

Now Veee spoke. "That is because here in the trail different folk can communicate, though their home languages are completely different. When I visited Tod's home, he became totally unintelligible."

"And she became ghostlike," Tod said. "We can truly associate with each other only here on the trail."

"That is interesting. It seems this trail is remarkable in diverse respects."

"It is," Veee said. "Be very careful what you eat here; some fruits are sickening. I can eat only red berries, and Tod can eat only blue berries. We think that is gender-related. We do not know what you might safely eat." She paused, "Assuming you do eat."

"I do eat, yes, in my fashion," Bem agreed. "I heed your warning."

"You came up this steep trail?" Veee asked, looking dubiously down it.

"Yes. It was no problem. That might be more of a challenge for your type, however."

"Yes. We would have trouble remaining on it without falling," Veee said.

"I have excellent traction," Bem said. "I will demonstrate." It slid to the edge and down the steep slope, remaining vertical. Its bottom surface seemed glued to the rock. Then it slid back up, with no motion of legs.

Tod and Veee stared, amazed. "What makes you go?" Tod asked.

"I have internal caterpillar treads." That was surely not the terminology, but the trail translated it to an approximation Tod could understand.

"Dry snail motion," Veee said, evidently hearing it in her own terms. "Remarkable."

"Just how far does it go?" Tod asked, intrigued. "Could you climb a vertical slope?"

"Of course. My land is challenging in spots."

"If there should be such a challenge ahead on the trail, would you help us to pass it?"

"Yes. That would initiate an exchange of favors."

Ah. "We will try to safeguard you if you eat and become ill, if we know how."

"Merely ensure than no predators attack me when I am unable to defend myself."

"We can try. We have as yet seen no predators here."

"If I comprehend correctly, the two of you are amenable to traveling with me to explore the trail."

"Yes," Veee said. "We do not know why we were summoned here, but we are interested, and wish to discover where the trail leads before we return to our homes."

"That aligns with my position. Let us then proceed."

They resumed motion along the trail, now walking on either side of Bem. Its internal tractor treads moved it along quite efficiently, the hide stretching smoothly to move back on the ground and forward where not in contact.

"May I make an observation?" Bem asked.

Tod smiled. "Feel free."

"The two of you are humanoid in form, yet you seem sapient. This strikes me as remarkable."

"There are humanoids in your world, but they are not intelligent?" Tod asked.

"They are animals. They forage and feed and mate without much organization. They do not converse linguistically, in the manner you do."

"Monkeys," Tod suggested.

Bem considered. "Yes, your term applies. I apologize for mistaking you for them."

Tod laughed. "We mistook you for a bug-eyed monster."

"Is that species sapient?"

"It is not generally considered to be so," Tod said.

"Then it seems we are equivalent in our misapprehensions."

"Yes," Tod agreed, smiling.

The mountainous terrain leveled out, and became a dense jungle of snakelike trunks interspersed by patches of multicolored moss. Tod wondered whether the same rule applied to that: blue edible for males, red for females. They might have to experiment, in due course.

"There is something aware of us," Bem remarked. "Several."

Tod felt a nervous chill. He had been able to accept the odd alien creature, as it was openly displayed and communicative, but the thought of something unknown bothered him. "Animals?"

"They seem to be of your general type," Bem agreed. "Four projecting limbs, a head knob, orifice with teeth. Also a tail. They proceed on the ground, through the brush on either side of the trail."

Veee lifted her nose and sniffed. "Now I wind them. Wolves or monkeys."

Tod saw and smelled nothing. Evidently the others had better senses than he did. Now he was glad he had the gun, though he would not use it except in real emergency.

Bem slowed. "I am feeling less sanguine," it said. Indeed, its colors were fading.

"It's the sickness," Veee said immediately.

"But you haven't eaten anything," Tod protested.

"I have been feeding," Bem said. "My skin attracts small particles from the air, absorbs the edible ones, and sloughs off the dust. It is a continuous process, which I can enhance by spreading my mantle." It spread small wings of skin from its shoulder region.

"Then you haven't eaten much," Veee said. "With luck you won't get very sick, and it will pass in a few hours. But you must stop eating now."

"I eat automatically as food touches my surface. That must be washed off with clean water."

"I hear a stream ahead," Veee said. "Can you make it there?"

"No." Bem turned gray and sank into the shape of an amorphous blob.

Now Tod heard the predators coming closer. They sensed meat.

He quickly unpacked the canvas bucket. "I will fetch water."

"But we must guard Bem from the wolfkeys," Veee said.

Wolfkeys? Maybe that fit. "All right. I'll guard Bem while you use this to fetch clean water." He paused. "Do you have a weapon?"

She showed a stone blade with a wickedly sharp edge. She had to have had it with her all along, yet he had never seen it before. He was glad that he had treated her courteously when they slept together; she was obviously not helpless. Then she was off with the bucket, running fleetly.

Tod got out his own knife. Then he dug out the gun, just in case. He made sure the clip was in place and it was functional. "If the wolfkeys attack, I may make a loud noise," he warned Bem. "Do not be alarmed; it is to defend us."

But Bem was now a puddling gray mound on the trail. It was sick, all right.

The predators came closer, showing themselves. They did indeed resemble wolves and monkeys, with large front teeth and what looked like prehensile tails. They did not approach closely, yet, evidently assessing the situation. Could this prey be overwhelmed?

Tod flashed his knife. This was his favorite: open oval shaped handle with finger ridges to protect his hand, four inch blade with a straight edge on one side and sharp serrations on the other. He had never used it in combat, but knew that it could do enormous damage to flesh in a hurry. And if that wasn't enough, the gun.

The predators, evidently impressed by his stance, stayed back. They clearly preferred helplessness in prey.

Veee returned, toting the filled bucket. It was heavy, but she was strong. He remembered those muscles she had. The wolfkeys had evidently been wary of her too, surely for good reason.

"Splash it on Bem," Tod said.

She let fly with the water. It inundated Bem and flowed across the trail. Bem's hide looked cleaner, and its colored stripes showed faintly.

"I think that helps," Tod said. "I'll fetch a second bucket, to be sure."

"Keep your knife handy," she said, gazing at it with open admiration. She knew a good weapon when she saw it. Hers was good too, but stone was no match for steel.

"Stay alert," he told her. "If they attack, scream and I'll run back."

"They won't attack." She glared at the closest wolfkey, and it backed off a step. Veee must have had experience with wild animals, and they knew it.

Tod hurried to the river where it crossed the trail, dipped out a bucketful, and hurried back. Veee remained on guard, her hair wild, her stone knife menacing. The predators were still lurking, but still not daring to attack. Had they charged in a mass, they might have won the day, but they did not seem to realize that. Unless they knew that the attempt would bring Tod charging back, making the effort more dangerous.

He sloshed the water on Bem, and it seemed to help further. The colors brightened, and the shape became closer to the original one.

They waited for the healing process to progress. "You are doing well," Tod told her. "I like that."

She glanced sidelong at him. He realized that her brown eyes matched her hair perfectly. "Are you trying to make me want it sooner?"

He laughed, not pretending to misunderstand. "No, my appreciation is honest. I am merely gaining respect for you." But he did regret that his illness had preempted what might have been the right moment before.

"The men in my land do not like women who stand up for

themselves."

"Actually, there are men in my land with a similar attitude. But we are in a mysterious and sometimes dangerous place, and we all need to stand up for ourselves and each other. You are the kind of woman I prefer to have here."

"You are close to succeeding."

"I wasn't trying to— " He broke off. "Are you teasing me?"

Veee considered. "I thought I was merely informing you of my state, but maybe I was flirting. I am not good at this sort of thing. I apologize."

"Don't! It becomes you." Then he reconsidered, as she had. "You don't need to tell me of your exact state of mind. A woman is entitled to her privacy. When you—if you—come to want it, all you have to do is kiss me, and I'll know. Meanwhile, just be yourself. I will respect you regardless."

She blushed, which was rare for her. "Very close."

Tod found himself getting aroused. If she was truly ready—

"Is this courtship?" Bem asked. It was close to its original shape and colors. "I inquire because though I know that multi-gendered creatures can have elaborate mechanisms for advising each other of their readiness to copulate, I have not seen it in practice and may misinterpret the signals."

Both of them made guilty starts. "Yes, I think it is," Tod said.

"In my frame, humanoids simply come together and interpenetrate. There is very little art to it."

"You are interested in art?" Veee asked.

Bem made a coruscation of light flashes, evidently laughter. "Our society is made of art. Without art we would not exist as superior beings. I myself am an architect."

"That's an art," Tod agreed. "You build cathedrals?"

It took Bem a moment to assimilate what was evidently an unfamiliar term. "I arrange patterns," it said.

"I'm not sure that's the same."

"It is as close as this common language can make it," Bem said. "Your architects may construct edifices of stones. Ours dictate patterns of animate flowers."

"Like sand pictures?" Veee asked.

Again Bem had to assimilate a term that was not quite right. "This may be a fair analogy," it agreed after a pause.

Veee returned to business. "In our distraction of courtship, we were neglecting you."

"You were guarding me," Bem reassured her. "The wolfkeys would have had me by now, otherwise."

"We made a deal. We are all helping each other."

"I appreciate that."

"But if the air makes you sick," Veee said, "how will you live? You have to eat."

"That is true," Bem said. "But a little food is coming to me now, and yet I am improving. Perhaps it was merely a bad section we passed through."

"Let's hope so," Tod said. "You do look better. Are you able to travel again?"

"Yes, though my pace may be slow at first."

Tod attached his knife sheath to his belt and put the knife in it. He wanted it close at hand as long as the predators were near. Veee's blade disappeared, leaving him quite curious where, but he decided not to ask.

They resumed motion, and the wolfkeys paced them. What were the predators expecting, now that Bem was recovering?

Now the trail crossed the river and moved into an open grassy plain. Patches of colored berries grew there. Tod and Veee paused to pick and eat some: blue for him, red for her. They were very good.

The predators came through the section, slinking from patch to patch for concealment. They still had not given up. That bothered Tod. Their group had successfully fended off the predators, and now that their ailing member was recovering health, they would be less vulnerable than before. The wolfkeys were surely aware of that. Why, then, were they wasting their time and effort maintaining the chase?

In due course the plain gave way to more mountains, but there was a level access between them, winding around their slopes. Maybe a river had carved it in the distant past. Still the wolfkeys followed, becoming more bold.

"Do they know something we don't?" Veee asked a trifle grimly.

"It is getting late in the day. We will have to stop to eat, and to sleep," Tod said. "Maybe they count on swarming us when we sleep."

"We can keep walking through the night if we have to."

"But eventually we'll have to rest."

"This terrain resembles that of my home world," Bem remarked. "If so, we will have a safe retreat."

Tod hoped so.

The route between mountains opened out into a glade replete with many berry bushes. They paused and ate, while Bem seined the air. They caught up on natural functions, then, refreshed, marched on.

So did the predators.

The mountains closed in again. The path became the bottom of a cleft between overlapping mountains, buttressed by sheer vertical walls on either side. They towered some fifty feet to the regular mountain slopes.

Then the trail ended. "Oh, no!" Tod exclaimed. "Box canyon."

"And the wolfkeys knew," Veee said. "This is their hunting

territory."

Indeed, the predators had closed in behind them, blocking the retreat. The trap had sprung.

"We can fight our way out," Tod said.

"There are too many of them."

"Not for a semi-automatic pistol."

Veee looked blank, and Bem's lights rippled in confusion. Neither had heard of this instrument.

Tod brought it out. "It shoots out metal bullets that puncture flesh, strikes key organs or bones, and kills. I can take out a dozen in short order, if I have to."

"This would not be effective against me," Bem said. "I have no organs or bones." It demonstrated by forming several holes in its torso.

That was interesting. Bem was truly a different form of life.

"But you're our friend," Veee said.

"Yes. But if the wolfkeys resemble me in flesh, if not in structure, they will not be stopped by it."

"They don't," Tod said. "They resemble us. That's why they're wary of knives. If we cut them, they will bleed. I'm sure bullets will hurt them similarly."

"There is no need," Bem said. "We can climb the wall where they can not go, to safety for the night."

"You can," Tod said. "Not us."

"My return favor. I will carry you up, one at a time."

"You really can do it?"

"Yes, now that I have regained my strength."

"Then take Veee up while I guard the base."

"Get on my backside," Bem told Veee. "Hold on to the skin. You will not hurt me."

Veee took hold of its skin. Her fingers sank in, gaining firm purchase. She raised one leg and dug in a toe, then the other. "I'm ready."

Bem glided to the wall and pressed its front side against it. Then it glided on up, carrying Veee.

Tod shook his head, bemused. This was a bem carrying a maiden away, and she was going willingly. The sci-fi junk he had seen would have a fit. Not that he had ever understood why bems chased luscious human damsels; what could they want with them, other than to consume their tender meat? Yet wouldn't that mean they would carry away fat folk instead? They never did.

The wolfkeys, seeing their prey unexpectedly escape, howled and charged.

Tod aimed his pistol and fired. The lead predator fell, but the others continued advancing. He shot again, and a second fell. Then a third. They were definitely made of flesh, bones, nerves, and blood.

They finally got the message, and retreated, leaving their companions to die alone.

Meanwhile, Bem achieved the top and deposited Veee there. It then compacted into a ball, rolled off the ledge, and plunged to the canyon floor. Tod stared in helpless horror as it bounced and settled. What a horrible accident!

Then Bem reformed into its normal shape, unharmed. "A faster descent," it explained.

"You were not fooling about having no bones or organs!"

"True. I cannot be damaged by impact. But if the predators had consumed my flesh, I would have suffered."

Surely so! Tod climbed onto Bem's backside, grabbing comfortable handholds, and they proceeded up the wall.

Tod had never been particularly nervous about heights, but did feel exposed as he rose up the vertical slope. Could Bem really hold securely onto the blank face of the cliff? Obviously it could, because it had carried Veee up. Still, it seemed precarious.

He craned his head to look back and down. The wolfkeys were gone, except for the three dead ones. They had learned the hard way about this particular prey. So the three travelers had not been doomed, regardless of Bem's ability. Still, it might have been a long way around to recover the trail without climbing. Assuming the trail was still here.

And there was a mystery: why would they be invited to follow a trail that dead-ended in a trap? Surely there were easier ways to foil the wolfkeys. No, they must have strayed from the trail and taken an offshoot. In which case they might have to retrace their route to locate it.

They reached the top. Bem slid smoothly around the bend and Tod was clinging to a horizontal blob. He let go, stepped off, and stood. "Thank you," he said, somewhat inadequately.

"It was the return favor."

"Maybe we will exchange more favors in the future."

"To mutual benefit," Bem agreed.

Veee was there, disheveled but pretty. Tod had not been impressed by her appearance at first, but of course she had been puking her guts out. Now she was a woman he knew and increasingly respected. That made a subjective difference. She was gazing at something. Tod looked.

The ground here was a moderate slope. And on it was the trail, plainly marked. Which meant they had not strayed; this was the correct route.

"What do you make of this?" Veee asked.

"I'm not much of a believer in coincidence. It seems we were intended to climb the wall. Whatever brought us here is putting us though our paces."

"This is my thought," she agreed.

"And mine," Bem said. "We have been rendered interdependent."

"Dependent on each other," Tod agreed. "As though we are members of a team that can't fully function with any of us missing."

Veee nodded agreement. Bem flashed a band of light that seemed to concur.

It was getting dark. Tod unpacked the little tent. He did not ask Veee whether she wanted to share it, knowing she would. With luck she might even conclude that their time had come, though that seemed doubtful in the presence of another sapient entity.

"What are you doing?" Bem asked.

"It gets cold at night, and sometimes rains," Tod said, though he had not yet seen rain here. But if there were rivers, there must be falling water. "We prefer to sleep in comfort, so I am putting up a shelter. I doubt there is room for you also, but we can try it and see."

"There is no need."

"Then just the two of us."

"No need for your shelter," Bem clarified.

Tod had learned to take the alien seriously. "Why not?"

"Because I can more readily provide what you require."

"How so?"

"Dispose yourselves for your slumber, and I will demonstrate."

Tod exchanged a glance with Veee. Then they lay down on the top of the unassembled tent, in their clothing, side by side.

Bem glided up, thinned, and spread itself over them like a thick soft warm blanket. "This is relaxing for me also," it said. "It is my estivation state."

Amazed, Tod took Veee's hand. She squeezed it, sharing his surprise. Obviously there would be no sex, regardless of their preference, but this was so easy he didn't mind. Then they slept, in perfect comfort.

CHAPTER 3: VAMPIRE

Tod woke refreshed, still holding Veee's hand. Had they never let go of each other during the night? They must have, to turn over, so as not to get cramped. That suggested that she had taken it again. Which in turn suggested that she had come to her decision.

He squeezed her hand lightly, in a kind of query. She squeezed back more firmly, in a kind of affirmation. Yes!

Bem drew itself off them and coalesced into its normal shape. Todd noticed that its color was now sand gray, emulating the ground on which they lay. Bem had camouflaged itself and them, protecting them from observation by possible hostile flying creatures. This was one versatile creature.

They foraged for breakfast, while Bem returned to its candy stripe colors and stood and seined the air for its own sustenance. There were fruiting trees in the vicinity, with an array of colors. Tod gathered blue, Veee red, and it was all right.

"When we have time alone?" he inquired as they returned with their burdens tucked into their shirts so as to leave their hands free. It made her look remarkably full breasted. He was determined to give her complete freedom of choice, though he was now desperately eager.

She did not need to guess his meaning. "I desire, but am not sure it is wise. It is not easy to ask. It would be easier if you simply required it. I would have no trouble obeying."

"That would nullify the point by eliminating your decision."

"Yes. But I am not accustomed to making such a decision for myself. My options have been limited to trying to avoid some men and being available to others." She flashed a self-disparaging smile. "Not always successfully, in either case. It is difficult for me to take such a step."

And he wanted that step. "When you are ready," he said, concealing his disappointment.

She took his hand. "I am I think teasing you, and I do not wish to do that. I know you want me, and I want to oblige, but I can't quite say it. Not when I am bound to mean what I say. Maybe I could more readily do so after you took me."

"That would be cheating, for us both."

"Yes," she agreed forlornly.

Soon they resumed traveling along the trail. It wound down the slope into a marsh where some crocodile-like creatures eyed them speculatively but did not venture onto the dry path. Was another predator trap approaching?

In the center of the swamp another branch of the trail intersected theirs. "If I understand this correctly," Tod said, "Each branch brings another participant. If we wait a bit, we may discover who or what comes along this one."

"It might not be friendly," Veee said.

"Then I'd rather meet it face to face, and deal with it immediately, than have it behind us."

She nodded. "You are bolder than I, and more sensible."

Tod glanced at Bem. "What do you say?"

"You wish my opinion?"

"You are one of us. We have shared favors. We trust each other. Yes, I want your opinion. It may be better than mine."

"I appreciate your confidence. I agree with you. I suspect it will be a creature unlike the rest of us, not hostile, but perhaps perplexed by the novelty of the trail. We may be able to assist it in understanding the cautions. Then perhaps we will become a party of four."

"To befriend it," Veee said. "As we befriended each other."

"We all face an unknown prospect," Tod said. "Something evidently wants us here, and wants us to work together. I am more curious than apprehensive. I want to resolve the mystery before I return home to my own world."

"My life at home was dull, often burdensome, even before my shame," Veee said. "Gathering tubers, carrying them in to the village pot. Serving any man who wanted. It has been otherwise on the trail. I think I do not want to go home."

Tod looked at her. "Whatever the mission or challenge we face here, if you remain, I think I want to remain too."

She blushed. "No man ever said that to me before."

"No woman ever expressed the interest in me that you have. I'm not handsome or rich or smart."

"I'm not delicate or high-breasted with fair hair."

"You are strong, useful, and look good enough."

"You warmed me when I was cold."

"You were very pleasant to warm."

"This courtship protocol is fascinating," Bem said.

"I guess you have nothing like it," Tod said, vaguely amused. "Being nonsexual."

"That is not true. We do have sexual interaction, as each individual is capable of mating with another."

"But no courtship?" Veee asked.

"When one of my kind encounters another, we decide rationally whether we wish to form a union," Bem said. "If we do, we do. It is straightforward. There is none of this charmingly oblique dialogue. Why is it that you do not come straight to the point?"

Tod considered. "To us, a marital commitment is no casual thing. Each person has myriads of aspects of individuality that may or may not be compatible with another person. So we come at each other subtly, trying to establish our needs and feelings and abilities, so that we can ascertain how suitable we are for each other without making a premature commitment. Sex is an important part of that, so we are especially cautious there."

"So if an esthetic female of your species offered you immediate sex, you would not indulge?"

"Exactly. Men always want it, but the implied commitment may be considerable. I will not be casually seduced."

"As I have ascertained," Veee agreed. "It becomes you."

"Bullshit."

Tod and Veee whirled around, and Bem's band of light circled its head to orient on the newcomer. They had been distracted by the dialogue, and not continued to observe the intersecting trail.

A woman stood there. She had what was best described as an hourglass figure, black hair so voluminous that it framed her whole tightly clothed torso, and a pretty face marred only by bright red pupils and formidable fangs. "Did you say the ugly word I thought I heard?" Tod asked.

"Bullshit is bullshit however phrased. What you said is completely and naively false. I, or any of my kind, could in the course of fifteen minutes enchant you, seduce you, drink your blood, and make you forget it ever happened, temporarily or permanently."

Tod took a breath and opened his mouth, uncertain what caustic response was about to emerge.

"Perhaps we should introduce ourselves before this proceeds further," Bem said diplomatically. "I am Beobrumemmik, of Snalliverti, colloquially known as Bem."

"I am Tod Timmins, of contemporary Earth," Tod said, following Bem's lead. That was probably best.

"I am Veee, of a land I can't identify because I do not know how it relates to the others."

"And I am Vanja, of the Vampire clan. I spied this trail, and it tempted me, so I took it, and now I am here. Shall we continue on our separate ways, having discovered nothing of mutual interest?"

"We suspect that we are being gathered here for some purpose," Tod said, maintaining tight control of his irritation. She had surely been trying to make him react, and he was determined not to give her that satisfaction. "The trail beckoned each of us, as it did you, but there are some dangers along it that seem to make a group safer than individuals might be."

"Pooh. What I can't handle, I can escape. Why should I want companions, aside from their blood?" Evidently modesty and subtlety were not parts of her character.

"Some foods are poisonous," Veee said. "And there are some ranging predators. We don't know what else."

"I feed on blood." Vanja flashed a toothy smile. "Not generally that of friends. I catch animals, and take only what they can reasonably spare. Few even realize they have been tapped, and if they do, they are not averse to repeating donations. As for predators, if they are land-bound I can escape them." She shrank into the form of a large bat, hovered in the air a moment, then returned to human form, snug clothing intact. "Why should I need any of you?"

Tod stared. She really was a classic vampire! But those were creatures of fantasy; how could she be here in the real realm? "Um."

"Intelligent observation," Vanja said sarcastically. "Are you looking at my teeth or my torso?"

Both, actually; she had caught him there. "You're a made-up spook, adapted from the unreasoning peasant's fear of bats and rabies," Tod said. "That trick you just showed us is impossible; for one thing it violates the equivalence of mass. So what are you, really? An illusion?"

Vanja gazed at him assessingly. "So you do not believe your eyes or ears. What evidence of my reality would you find persuasive, not that I care much for your ignorant opinion?"

"Seduce him and make him forget it," Veee said. "Within fifteen minutes."

Vanja smiled. "You're his woman? For such a thing I will require his direct permission as well as yours. It's a matter of professional ethics."

What a bluff! He called it. "You have my permission. Do your thing."

"Mark your timepiece."

Tod wore a watch with an elapsed time bezel he seldom used. He set it at the current minute and stood there waiting on her, but nothing happened. She did not even approach him. "When you're ready," he said, irritated.

Vanja laughed. So, oddly did Vee, and Bem made a musical chime. What was so funny?

"It has been done," the vampiress said.

"What has been done? You never touched me."

"Check your underpants."

What irrelevance was this? He checked.

His undershorts were on backwards.

How could that be? He had had them on correctly, because he had urinated not long ago and had no trouble with their fly.

"Feel your penis."

Perplexed, he reached into his shorts. His member was flaccid and damp. In fact it was spent, as if it had just ejaculated.

"Look at your timepiece."

He looked at his watch. Fifteen minutes had passed.

Faced with this evidence, he had to yield the point, to a degree. "Exactly what did you do with me? Hypnotize me into believing an illusion?"

"You will soon remember, as the potion wears off."

Tod looked at Veee. She gravely nodded. "She did you," she murmured. "My fault; I asked her to."

He looked at Bem. "True. She approached you, undressed you, aroused you, and copulated with you while you were standing, so to speak. Then she dressed you. She bit you slightly on the neck, then resumed her former stance."

"To make you forget," Vanja said. "For a few minutes. A small injection, and just a taste of your blood. A love bite, really, not a feeding bite."

Tod felt his neck. There was a small painless welt that had not been there before.

Then the memory began to return. Indeed, she had approached him and stripped him. Somewhere along the way her clothing disappeared. She had kissed him on the neck, except that now he knew it had been the bite. He had stood unmoving, not cooperating, but when she had his pants off she had touched his penis with her extremely evocative fingers and made it stiffen instantly. Then she had wrapped her arms about his upper torso, lifted herself against him, wrapped her legs around his waist, and somehow set her open cleft down on his member, taking it in. She had kissed him on the mouth with seeming passion, her fangs retreating to mere eyeteeth, and squeezed inside, and he had erupted, ejaculating violently into her. Then she had lifted herself off, dropped to the ground, cleaned out the dripping ejaculate, and put his undershorts on him backwards. Then his trousers, forwards. And returned to her present place.

And Veee had seen it all.

Worse, perhaps, it meant the vampire had not been fooling about her ability to control males. He felt a muted passion for her that only his present depleted state suppressed. If she demanded a repeat performance, he would be overwhelmingly tempted to oblige.

Vanja faltered. She wavered on her feet, caught herself, and wavered again. Then she faced to the side and vomited.

Veee went to her, producing a cloth to wipe her face. "It is the sickness," she said. "Sit down; it will pass."

"But how?" the vampiress asked between heaves.

"You sipped his blood. We each sickened after first eating here. It seems that blood is not right for you, here on the trail; you must avoid it."

"I am weak," Vanja moaned. "And cold."

"The blanket," Veee snapped to Tod.

He dug it out of his pack and brought it to her. Veee wrapped it around Vanja's shoulders. But now the woman was shivering violently.

"Body heat," Veee said. "Tod?"

"I don't want to get close to her!" Tod protested. "If I do—" He glanced downward, indicating his concealed penis, which was coming back to life.

"Bem," Veee said.

Bem glided there, became the warm blanket, and wrapped itself around Vanja. "Oh, that helps," she murmured gratefully.

Evidently Bem could control the heat, because a wisp of steam rose from the outer fringe. Vanja's chill soon ameliorated. She looked blissful.

"Your clothing," Veee said. "What happened to it?"

The vampiress smiled. "I wear no clothing. It interferes with my conversion and seduction. I merely color my skin appropriately." She extended a white forearm, and in a moment it turned dark blue, with a sleeve line at the wrist. It looked just like a skintight shirt.

"That is my kind of ability," Bem said, his surface turning polka dotted.

"Barely the shadow of yours," Vanja said. "I can't do shape or heat. Not beyond my bat form, or the natural heat of my body."

"And your fangs," Bem said.

"Them too," she agreed, her fangs expanding into tusks, then retreating to obscurity.

"Still, we can surely get along."

"Maybe we can. I truly appreciate your gift of warmth, Bem, and must say that you, Tod, are a good fuck. I may want to screw you again, when I recover."

"Do you have to use the crudest terms?" Tod asked. "I realize that the ambiance of the trail is translating them, but they remain obnoxious in mixed company."

Vanja smiled. "I rephrase: you are a good lover, and it would be no burden to indulge with you again."

"Thank you," Tod said with mixed feelings. They had not made love, because there had been no love in it; she had indeed screwed him. But he preferred polite euphemism.

The vampire glanced at Veee. "Where do I stand with you?"

"Stand where you choose," Veee said guardedly.

"May I speak with candor?" As if she had not been doing so unmercifully throughout.

"Yes," Veee said tightly.

"I seduced your man in front of you, and you know now that I can take him from you any time I choose, and that I lack much conscience in this respect. To me, your kind is prey."

"Yes."

"Yet when I sickened, you were the first to help me. You diagnosed it, and are treating it, making the others cooperate. You could have killed me in my weakness, or at least banished me. You could have been rid of me, and you knew it. Even now you could tell Bem to unwrap me and let me shiver, and Bem would do it."

"Yes."

"Why are you helping me?"

"We are being summoned here for a reason. We do not know why, but we will surely need all that are called. Your role must be honored."

"Even at the sacrifice of your man?"

Veee winced, but answered gamely enough. "If that is the price of it."

"Perhaps. I think you have a soft heart."

Veee's mouth quirked. "Yes."

"And an honest nature."

"Yes," Veee said, almost smiling.

"I want you for a friend."

Now Veee frowned. "I did not offer that."

"If you treat me this well when you don't like me, you will be well worth my time when you do. Already I know I can trust you with my life."

Tod saw that the vampire was a pretty shrewd judge of character. But where was she going with this?

"I do not want to be your friend," Veee said. "I wish I had not dared you to seduce Tod. I thought you were bluffing."

"Never doubt the word of a vampire. But you are right to put a price on your friendship. I must buy it."

"Friendship can not be bought!"

Vanja smiled, her fangs flashing. "Anything can be bought, if the price is right."

"I have no price!"

The vampire considered briefly. "We shall see. I will start by giving you back your man, or as much of him as is feasible."

"Feasible?"

"There are stories about vampires, often more exaggerated than accurate, yet usually with a kernel of truth. Such as that anyone bitten by a vampire later becomes one."

Tod nodded. He had heard that. Now he was worried, because she had bitten him.

"Here is that kernel," Vanja continued. "Anyone bitten by a vampire retains an interest, because of the hormones used to pacify them for the act. Women want to associate, to be friends. Men want to have sex. So there is a kind of conversion, but not to the vampire state. If I mated with Tod and produced offspring, they would be vampires; that's how new vampires are made. Reproduction, not corruption. I have no intention of becoming impregnated, however, so it is academic. But his urge to be with me will inevitably grow, as long as he is in my presence, and I will be inclined to oblige it. We vampires are lusty folk."

"Then you can't give him back," Veee said, more tightly.

"I can do so to an extent, in this manner: by telling you how to hold him, so that he is as attracted to you as he is to me. I realize this is half a loaf, but it is the best I can offer. The seed of desire has been planted in him, and it will not be denied. But we can share him, especially if we are friends. There need be no rivalry, merely understanding and acceptance."

"How can we share him?"

"Don't I have a choice here?" Tod asked.

"No," both women said together.

"You must seduce him now, before the seed expands further," Vanja said. "That share of him you win will remain yours, and will not be subject to further erosion. He will love us both."

"Now?" Veee asked, dismayed.

"Time is of the essence. I urge you not to waste it."

"But how can you want to share him?"

Vanja shrugged within the blanket. "He is not as important to me as he is to you. I am not the commitment kind; I normally have a number of enamored men around me. He is a mere dalliance I will oblige because there is no other man here and I need the attention of a man. It is easy for me to share; my feeling toward him does not approach yours."

"Mine?"

"You are on the verge of love."

Tod could see by Veee's pained reaction that the vampire had scored.

"Then it must be," Veee said.

"You have not yet seduced him. For this purpose you must not wait on his decision; you must take him now. Your initiative is important."

"So I gather. But I am not accustomed to taking the initiative. In my society initiative is almost by definition male. I got in trouble for it when I tried."

"You are no longer in your society," Vanja said firmly. "Here the rules are different, as I discovered the difficult way when I tasted his blood. We both must adapt"

"True," Veee agreed reluctantly. "But though I am not now in my society, my society remains in me. It is not my nature to act in such a manner."

"How badly do you want him?" Vanja asked shrewdly.

Again Veee was plainly suffering. "I do want him."

"Then it is merely a matter of means, not of ends. You must take him."

"I don't know how!" Veee wailed, frustrated.

Vanja contemplated her as she might a grazing but alert deer, assessing ways and means. "Do you dance?"

"I was never good at that. My proportions are wrong."

"I am good at it. In fact it was my secret vice, because I refused to limit myself to the dowdy traditional movements. I dance for the sheer pleasure of it, but it can be seductive too. I will teach you."

Veee grimaced. "You can't change my shape."

"Your shape will do, properly enhanced. You have significant physical assets. Come here."

Veee paused, considering, then went to the blanketed vampire. They conversed in whispers.

"Are you sure?" Veee asked when she had heard what Vanja had to say. She was clearly amazed.

"Reasonably. Try it and see."

"But never in my life did I think to try that! I envied the dancers, but would have been punished had I openly copied their motions."

"How many times must I say it? You are not where you came from. The rules are different here, and your need is immediate."

Veee nodded thoughtfully. "Give me time to prepare." She walked back along the trail.

"What is going on?" Tod asked plaintively.

"The courtship will intensify," Bem said. "Veee realizes that she can no longer wait for mutual agreement. She must act now. You should remove your clothing to facilitate the culmination."

"This is ridiculous!" But Tod did doff his clothing, realizing that he valued Veee and wanted her to have her best chance. If she lost him, he would also lose her.

"This is necessity," Vanja said. "I would not have bitten you had I anticipated this complication."

"Complication?"

"That I would want Veee's friendship. I would have seduced you without biting you, though that would not have made you forget. My error."

"If I may inquire, during this pause," Bem said. "What made you take the trail?"

"Two of us vied for the favor of the vampire chief. My rival seduced him first. That made me outcast and unwelcome, since my presence would be a threat to the chief's new wife. Especially since I had danced for him, and he would soon want more of that. I had to depart and find a new swarm. That was not a pleasant prospect. Then I saw the trail."

"But the trail was empty."

"It could lead to another community of vampires. Failing that, to villages of normal people, good for sustenance, and maybe some handsome men. I like sex almost as well as I like blood; it is my vampire nature." She smiled briefly. "Some stories claim we are cold-bodied, walking dead. In fact we are the opposite, hot in more than one respect. That's why I took the dare: it gave me a pretext to get a man into me without social complications. Or so I thought." She eyed Tod speculatively. "Fast is fun, but slow is better. I want to spend a night with you and keep you in me throughout while I dance."

"While you dance?" he asked, thinking he had misheard.

"Dancing is not limited to external. I will demonstrate. Maybe tonight."

Tod did not want to admit how wickedly that tempted him. "I would not be, um, firm enough to do that."

"We shall see." It was the same phrase she had used with Veee, evidently meaning that she knew better.

"I am curious," Bem said. "Does the ejaculate of a human male have similar appeal to you as his blood?"

"You are one smart entity," Vanja said. "Yes, its impact on a vampire is much like that of blood. When I seduce a man I acquire his semen, and that fulfills the same need that blood does, so to have him clasping me and delivering spurts of the divine essence is a continuing thrill. The beauty of it is that not only does a man not mind, he delights in making this contribution. I don't have to bite him to have pleasure of him."

Veee returned. She had harvested trailside grasses and fashioned a skirt that barely covered her bottom, and a halter that hung across her breasts. She was otherwise nude. The apparel, slight as it was, wholly changed her body, making her look utterly feminine. The vampire was right: Veee did have significant female assets. They had been de-emphasized before, to an extent; now they were being boldly promoted. She had in effect changed from housewife to harem girl. Vanja's advice had obviously been potent.

"Tod," Veee said. "I am courting you. Are you amenable?"

What could he say? "Yes."

Veee began to dance. The motion animated her. She had solid female parts, as he had known, but now her torso was alive in a new way. Her hips rolled in a kind of hula, and the grass provided shadowed views of her midsection as the blades swished from side to side. She turned, and her buttocks flashed through the skirt. It was just about the sexiest thing Tod had ever seen.

She completed her turn, and now her bosom bounced under the waving grass, the nipples peeking randomly out. The momentary winks were twice as intriguing as fully exposed flesh would have been. She shook her torso, and her breasts rippled, collided, and rippled back.

Tod discovered that he had an almost painfully stiff erection. What a show she was putting on! He had never imagined that she would be capable of it, considering her prior diffidence. She had to have known how, from observing dancing women in her home frame; the vampire had persuaded her to emulate those motions. What a transformation!

Now she was close, and the musky smell of her body further inflamed his passion. She stepped into him, her torso still gyrating. She caught his hands in hers and brought them behind her, setting them on her flexing buttocks. The touch was electric. His whole body seemed to be on fire with desire.

She nudged up against him, her breasts brushing his chest, then pressing possessively against it. She caught his head in her hands and brought it down to hers for an ardent kiss. She had kissed him before, but this was infinitely intensified.

"But do you really want it?" he gasped as it ended. He knew the answer, but wanted it on the record, as it were.

"Yes!" she pushed against him so that he had to step back, but one of her ankles hooked behind his, and he fell to the soft ground beside the trail. She was on him, kissing him again, her taut belly jammed against his. His hands were still on her bottom, feeling its muscular deformation as she pressed ever more closely against him.

Then he was sliding inside her hot crevice and hotter channel, plunging to full depth. He spurted into that hungry orifice, endlessly, as if he had not had sex for a year. "Oh, Veee!" he breathed.

"I love you." Then: "Your presence inside me excites me. Now I know that yours is the first penis I truly wanted there. Now I am coming too."

And she was. He felt her vagina tighten around him, pulsating, as the throes of her orgasm wracked her body. He was done with his, but this was a new and exciting experience for him, being there for hers, a thrill in its own right. She had truly wanted him, physically as well as emotionally. He found that transcendentally meaningful.

Finally they relaxed together. "Oh, Veee!" he repeated. "That was worth waiting for!"

Her orgasm had not made her lose track of the game. "And now how do you feel about Vanja?"

"I—still desire her," he said, surprised. "But I think I love you."

"That will do." She kissed him. "Now we should rejoin the others."

"We should," he agreed laughing. With the motion of his belly he realized that he was still pleasantly inside her.

She got off him, produced a cloth—where *did* she keep such items?—wiped him off, then herself. Then they found their clothes, dressed, and rejoined the others. They had never been out of sight of them, but this was a matter of attention rather than distance.

"Now he is half yours," Vanja said. "Excellent technique, I might add. I don't suppose you have any vampire ancestry?"

"None," Veee said, smiling. "We just happen to know how to do it, when we have reason. You gave me reason."

"All I did was tell you to emulate a dancer, in costume and motions. You learned rapidly and well."

"I knew I had to, after seeing you seduce him. Whatever I could do, I had to do now. So I did."

She certainly had, Tod thought. It was a one hundred and eighty degree turnabout from her former willing reticence. She had gone from pleading with him simply to take her, to taking *him*. But it also meant that the vampire was some teacher, when she tried. She had known what aspects to have Veee focus on. How to bring out the full illustrious *woman* in Veee.

"That was a most interesting demonstration," Bem said. "Vanja agrees; she found it stimulating."

"How do you know that?" the vampire asked sharply.

"You forget that I have been in close contact with you throughout. I felt your body responding, especially when she made him take hold of her posterior bifurcation and then took his copulatory projection into her pelvis."

"I did," she confessed. "When I dance I am transported. When I see a dance I live it myself. Similar for sex; I can't see it without feeling it. When she seduced him, I felt as if I were doing it myself. Oh that flowing sperm! I got wet."

"You did," Bem agreed.

"I think my chill is gone, and I am feeling better. You may unwrap me now."

Bem did, and Vanja stood naked. Then her painted apparel appeared, clothing her. Tod was amazed by how thoroughly that coloration changed her body, making it sexily decent instead of sexily exposed.

"Now we are four," Bem said, resuming his normal configuration and coloration. "Shall we proceed along the trail?"

"Might as well," Vanja agreed. She came to Tod and took his right hand. Veee, almost defensively, took his left. Tod was not sure how to react, but he found that he liked being the object of such attention.

"We can alternate nights," Vanja said to Veee.

"No, we can share."

"We will lie on either side of him, and alternate taking him in."

"Agreed."

"I'm glad you girls have decided my business," Tod said, attempting mild irony.

"Women always decide," Vanja said. "The difference is that now we are doing it openly."

"Where I come from, a man has one woman at a time. How can I handle two?"

"You are no longer where you come from," Veee said, echoing the essence of what the vampire had said to her.

"You can't 'handle' even one," Vanja said. "Go with the flow."

Tod pondered. He needed a rationale to enable him to be comfortable with two women at once, when he'd never really had one woman before. The prospect of endless sex excited him, but he feared mischief in the larger relationships. He had been on the verge of working it out with Veee; then Vanja had come on the scene and complicated it enormously.

"In my land," Veee said, "a chief may have one wife and several mistresses. Only the wife has authority."

"Mine too," Vanja agreed. "I was willing to be the mistress, but the wife feared I would win him over in time and become the wife." She laughed. "She was savvy in that respect."

"Man's wife better half," Tod quoted from memory, trying to make light of it. "Mistress better hole."

"She has to be, without legal standing," Vanja said. "Sex is her only claim on him."

And there was the answer. "Then I will think of Veee as my wife, and you as my mistress."

He waited for the explosion of outrage by one or both of them, but it didn't come. They were amenable?

It seemed they were. Veee had declared her love for him, and won her share of him. Vanja was less committed, willing to settle for a temporary affair before she moved on.

"Tod's blood made you sick," Veee said, changing the subject. "Yet he's not of this trail realm. It should have been an animal's blood that affected you."

"That's right!" Tod agreed. "Unless she's allergic to the blood of creatures not of her home frame."

"In which case I will starve," Vanja said wryly. "My term as mistress may be of brief duration."

"Unless the compatibility of the trail means that you can eat the blood of its creatures," Veee said. "Tod is from a different land. It may be only the blood of visitors that poisons you."

"I can soon find out." Vanja changed to bat form and flew away. Tod felt her hand become a claw before she let go.

They walked on in silence. Tod was uncertain what he hoped for. Objectively he suspected that he would be best off to be free of the vampire, but he did still hunger for sex with her, and did not like the thought of her dying. Probably Veee was wrestling similarly with her own conflicting feelings. Bem must be leaving it to them to work out, having no special stake in this triangle.

The trail came to another field of colored fruits. They stopped to eat their assigned colors.

The bat returned, and became Vanja. "I can eat local blood!" she exclaimed. "You set me straight, Veee."

"I am glad," Veee said.

"But again, you could have been rid of me, had it been otherwise. Why do you care?"

"I have come to know you somewhat. You are a person, with needs and feelings." Veee paused. "And you caused me to do what I had to do, to commit to Tod. I appreciate that."

"You are not much for jealousy, are you?"

"I am a realist. We can all get along, as we understand each other."

"I must win your friendship," Vanja said. "Not merely your tolerance. I think I want that more than I want the man."

"I have not agreed to that," Veee said.

Bem flashed merry colors. "You must court her, Vanja. She is slow to yield, but surely worth it when she does."

"Yes!" Tod breathed.

"Yet I wonder," Veee said, holding up a blue berry. "Have we assessed the situation correctly?" She was delicately changing the subject again.

"Don't eat that!" Tod said.

But Veee bit into it.

They all waited. Time passed, and she did not get sick.

Tod picked a red berry. He ate it. It was delicious. Nothing happened.

"We assumed that I consumed a cloud of bad air," Bem said. "But perhaps it was merely initial air."

"And we all get sick the first time we eat here, whatever it is, berries, air, blood, semen," Vanja said. "It is an initiation, an adaptation. Thereafter we belong."

"And because I am acclimatized to the environment of the trail," Tod said, "I am in effect part of its substance. You would have sickened had you tried the blood of any of us, or of a native creature. Assuming any creatures here are natives; they may all be imports, as we are."

"You saw the key, Veee," Vanja said. "You had the courage to risk an illness I know from experience you would not want to repeat. For the benefit of all of us. You have insight, courage, and loyalty."

"I just like to know what's what," Veee said modestly.

"I must have your friendship."

"You could bite me."

"I want it earned, not coerced. You are the best woman Tod or any man could have; you are the best friend any woman could have. I am a fair judge of character, and I know this already. I will do my best to win you. In the interim I will act toward you as a friend would act, trying to be in this respect the best I can be, hoping in time for your return sentiment."

Veee did not answer. What could she say? That she liked the prospect of sharing her man with a luscious seductive vampire, or befriending that same creature?

Then, amazingly, Tod saw a tear on Veee's cheek. Then he knew that Vanja had already won her case, though it might take time for the full realization of it. Veee, too, wanted a true friend, just as she wanted a true lover. She richly deserved both.

CHAPTER 4: WIZARD

The trail wound on through a highly varied landscape. It reached a large lake or sea whose water was pleasantly warm.

"I must test for predators," Bem said. It went to the edge, extended a fold of skin, and seined the water. "There is no predator near," it announced. "We can safely use this water."

"Thank you," Tod said. "It is a comfort to have your reassurance, after some of the dangers we have faced."

Bem made an appreciative band of colors around its knob.

"I want to bathe," Vanja said. "You must join me, Veee."

"Why?"

"Because I will go nude, and this will arouse the man. You must arouse him similarly, at least until his emotion sets and is constant. Thereafter I will be able to seduce him, but not seduce him from you. His desire will be evenly divided between us. This is the way it must be, so that we can share him without rancor." As she spoke, her painted clothing faded, leaving her bare. Tod wondered whether her jet black pubic hair was real, or more coloring. Did it matter?

Veee nodded. She doffed her robe and accompanied the vampire to the water.

Tod stayed back, watching them. Vanja's hourglass figure was supremely evocative from behind, as she had to know. But Veee's more solid form, with its powerful legs and muscular buttocks, was similarly evocative, as she too had to know. When she had donned the grass skirt...

His erection was straining at his clothing. What the hell. The girls were out to seduce him, and he was more than willing. He got out of his clothing and let his member stand tall.

Meanwhile Bem entered the water. It formed into a shape roughly like a giant skate or manta ray and swam with a kind of flying motion. Versatile creature!

Veee and Vanja waded in, then swam. They splashed each other laughing. Their breasts flashed as they leaped half out of the lake. Their hair, matted in the air, spread voluminously in the water, brown and black. Then, acting together, they swam on their backs, their legs toward him as they kicked high. Their junctures showed momentarily as the water rippled across them. They were openly tempting him.

"I think the only thing more intriguing than single courtship is double courtship," Bem remarked from its vantage to the side. "I believe they are inviting you to play."

"You bet!" Tod ran to the water and dived in, rushing to join the women.

They met him together. Veee flung her arms about him and pressed her breasts to his chest as she kissed him. Vanja ducked underwater, then came up against him facing away, her hands busy. In a moment she was feeding his stiff penis into her cleft and pushing her bottom back to take him all the way in. He climaxed immediately as Veee's kiss turned into tonguing. It was as though he were ejaculating into her, powerfully and wonderfully.

Then they released him and came up for air, in their fashions. They played with him, splashing him, racing him, teasing him, until he began to react again. Then Vanja kissed him from the side, caught his hands and set them on her breasts, while Veee wrapped her legs about him, leaned back, and took him in. It took longer, but they managed to make him climax again, marvelously. It was weird not penetrating the one he was kissing or fondling, but had its novelty and considerable appeal. He doubted that they were climaxing with him; it was more complicated for a woman. They were doing this as a challenge and to assert their dominance in this respect. They surely enjoyed making him respond, and that sufficed, at least for this occasion.

"I could get to like this," he gasped as his pulses ebbed.

"It's just the beginning," Vanja assured him, gently nipping his ear.

"We have plans for the night," Veee agreed.

Maybe that was when they would get their own climaxes. "I hope I survive them." All three laughed.

In due course they emerged, joyously clean. "I thought vampires were cold blooded," Tod said as they dried in the sunshine.

"In spirit, not body," Vanja said. "And hot-blooded when it comes to sex."

"I noticed."

"And you see, you don't have to choose between us," Vanja continued. "You can have us both, simultaneously."

"I noticed that too."

Dry, they dressed in their fashions and moved on along the trail, which continued along the shore.

Vanja sniffed the air. "Predator," she announced. "I'll investigate." She transformed to bat form and took off.

"I am surprised you, um, indulge so freely, after your prior caution," Tod said to Veee.

"I have to, to match her pace, lest she take a larger share of you. But I confess that this situation gives me leave to do things I would not have dared try alone. In my realm a forward woman is anathema."

That explained a lot. Veee had been loath to make any kind of sexual decision, until Vanja had become a catalyst. Now Veee was evidently enjoying being wanton. The pendulum might swing back the other way, in due course, but it was fun for now.

"You are getting to like her," Bem said.

"I am," Veee said seriously.

"There's something about her, apart from her expressed desire to be friends."

"Some affinity we have for our companions," Tod agreed. "I don't know exactly what it is, but we four have something in common."

"Disaffection with our home worlds," Veee said.

"That, too."

The bat returned and transformed. "Four-footed creatures, too many to balk."

"Wolfkeys," Veee said. "They pursued us before, but we escaped them. We need to find a safe retreat for the night." Because the day was getting late.

Tod looked out across the water. "There's an island. We could swim to it. Can the wolfkeys swim?"

"Surely they can," Vanja said. "Probably as well as we can."

"You could fly across and be safe," Veee reminded her.

"Only if I could thereby help the rest of you cross." The vampire pondered, then amplified: "I am not normally gregarious or loyal to a group, but I do settle my debts. You helped me when I was ill, and now I value the friendship, sex, and warmth you provide." She glanced at Veee, Tod, and Bem as she said the words. "So I have become committed."

Bem was sampling the water again. "Worse news: swimming predators have been alerted by our water sport, and are forging rapidly toward us. They seem to be large fish with electrical properties. I suspect they touch prey and shock it, stunning it, then tear it apart and consume it."

"Crossbreed of sharks and electric eels," Tod said.

"Shocks," Vanja suggested.

He smiled. "Shocks," he agreed.

"We are in trouble," Veee said. "If we swim, not only with the wolves following us, the shocks will intercept us. But there must be a way to escape them, as there was before. Assuming we were brought here for a reason."

Tod looked about. He saw no trees large enough to hold them. There was only the open beach and the water. "There may be a way," he said. "Desperate, dangerous, but possible."

"We are interested," Bem said with its typical understatement.

"Timing is of the essence. It's a matter of vectors. Vanja, can you scout the shocks and tell me how far away they are and what their swimming velocity is?"

She became the bat and flew out across the water.

"Bem, can you carry our clothing and supplies across to the island, using your skate form?"

"I can," Bem agreed.

"But Tod, the wolves will follow Bem to the island and attack there," Veee protested.

"Yes," he agreed. "They are surely very hungry by now. They won't hesitate. We'll swim across as a group, just ahead of them. I doubt they can swim faster than we can." He got out of his clothing again, and Veee removed hers, though she was obviously not at all easy about this.

Vanja returned and converted. "They are swimming twice as fast as we can, and will pass the island shortly."

"Good. I hear the wolves baying. The timing is about right."

Veee stared at him, but did not comment.

The first wolfkey came into view. Tod raised his arm as if pointing a gun. The creature skidded to a halt, then skulked behind a bush. Tod's pistol was part of the package Bem would transport, so he couldn't use it at the moment. With luck it would take the predators a while to discover that.

"So it's the same pack as before," Veee said.

"Can you operate your projectile pistol while swimming?" Bem asked. "I can return it to you for this purpose."

"No. I'm not sure it will operate in water. Now we must swim. Stay with the group; it's important that we be together."

"That will make it easier for the predators on either side to corral you and consume you," Vanja said. "I will swim with you, as there will be no point in my escaping alone."

Tod noted that once the vampire joined to the group, she was fully committed, even to the death. He liked that. His fascination with her body was one thing, but he was coming to appreciate her other qualities.

They entered the water together. Immediately the wolves charged. They splashed into the water without hesitation and started dog-paddling in pursuit.

Fortunately Tod's estimate had been correct: the wolves could swim no faster than the humans did. The two parties crossed the water toward the island almost in tandem, separated by only a few feet.

Halfway across, Tod turned to Vanja. "How close are the shocks now?"

She transformed and flew up ahead. In moments she was back. "They'll pass the island just after we reach it."

"Perfect! Keep swimming."

As they reached the shallow water around the island, Tod saw the white ripples of swiftly moving creatures just under the surface. "Get to your feet!" he called. "Wade ashore."

The three of them did, and Bem sailed up to the beach and slid onto it. The wolves were close behind.

Then the shocks arrived. There were howls of anguish as the electricity flowed, stunning the wolves.

The four of them stood and watched as the water frothed with the action. The wolves tried to fight, but they were out of their element. The water turned red with blood.

None made it to the island. Tod felt weak-kneed and exhilarated. He had played their cards as appropriately as he knew how, but had the timing been off...

"Ooh, Tod!" Veee cried, hugging him. "You did know!"

"A desperation ploy, as I said. We needed to time it so the wolves were still in the water when the shocks arrived. The shocks can't come after us on land, and with luck they will be sated and gone by tomorrow morning."

"Kiss him, Veee," Vanja said. "I'm going to."

"That spared me the necessity," Bem said. They all laughed.

There were berry bushes on the island. They picked and ate, then Tod pitched his little tent. "You girls can have that for the night."

"Thank you," Vanja said. Then both women grabbed him and

hauled him in with them. He found himself buried in warm flesh that was doing things to his face, torso, and groin simultaneously. They might be taking turns, but he was unable to tell whose orgasms he was sharing. It hardly seemed to matter. At least now they were getting their own climaxes; that much he could tell despite the pleasant confusion. It wasn't limited to him.

"But it would have been another matter, if we had gotten eaten in the water," Veee reminded him severely between kisses. "We would not have given you any of this." Obviously true.

"Or this," Vanja said, doing something indefinably naughty, even for her.

Eventually they let him sleep, his face cushioned against two or three soft breasts, his hands pinned between warm thighs. But they were at him again in the morning, bringing him off twice more, sharing equally.

"Remarkable," Bem said as they climbed out of the crowded little tent. "I am amazed by the continuing courtship variations."

"It's heaven," Tod said. "But much more of the same and it will be hell. There's only so much sex I can handle."

"We will decide when you have had enough," Vanja said.

Veee kissed his ear. "I love you," she whispered. That seemed more meaningful than all the rest.

Vanja had surely overheard, but she merely smiled, a trifle sadly. Her commitment was of a different nature. She did not begrudge Veee her emotion. Did vampires ever truly love?

Bem tested the water. "The shocks have gone," it announced. "But they remain in the vicinity, perhaps in the hope that we will soon reenter the water."

"We'll wait," Tod said. "Even if we have to talk about the weather."

"Is weather our concern?" Bem asked.

"It's humor. It seems we have time to pass, and will have to entertain ourselves. No, not with more sex," he added quickly as the two women approached him. "With dialogue. We surely have things to work out."

"Perhaps we can attempt to fathom our unifying theme," Bem suggested.

"Good idea." Tod looked around. "Any suggestions?"

"I have a thought," Veee said, somewhat hesitantly.

"Out with it, girl. In this little community we like forward women."

Veee blushed at the teasing. "I like to paint with sand. Tod likes to play music. Vanja likes to dance. Bem makes artistic structures. These are all arts. Could it be the arts that unify us?"

Tod felt his jaw trying to drop. "Yes! It could be."

Encouraged, Veee continued. "Because we are quite different kinds of people, and might not like each other well unless we have some common ground. We each appreciate the arts, and thus each other."

"Let's do it," Vanja said.

The others looked at her. "Do what?" Tod asked.

"Art. Put ours together and see how we like it."

"I don't know," Tod said.

But Veee was already getting on it. "Here is a sandy patch," she said. "A place."

"A stage," Tod said.

"A stage." She used her hands to sweep it clear, and her feet to form a roughly circular ridge of sand around it. "Tod, you must make music. Vanja, you must dance. Bem—" She broke off, stalled.

"I will form the props," Bem said.

Tod brought out his ocarina and began to play a melody.

Vanja stepped onto the stage and danced.

Bem formed into a bench-like mound.

Vanja danced to the side and took Veee's hand. "Oh, I can't dance," Veee protested. "Not artistically."

Vanja burst out laughing, and Bem made bright flashes. Even Tod was hard put to it to keep playing.

Vanja brought Veee to the bench and made her sit on it. Then she danced, addressing Veee like the object of courtship.

Tod shifted to a love song. The words did not come through, but the melody was evocative. *Alas my love you do me wrong, to cast me off discourteously...*

Vanja truly could dance. Her body was not trying to be seductive now, but pleading, focusing on Veee, openly begging for friendship. Every motion contributed to that appeal. She took Veee's hand and kissed it. Finally Veee consented, and Vanja bent low, kissed her face and fell swooning, her plea accepted.

It ended by mutual consent. They had all contributed to the impromptu presentation. Tod felt somehow fulfilled, and was sure the others did too. The arts did unify them.

Now if they could only figure out why they were here.

Bem tested the water again. "The shocks have gone too far away to be a present menace to us," it announced. "We can safely cross the water back to the mainland."

They did, swimming at greater leisure. Near the shore the girls waylaid Tod once more, doubly, as if to guarantee that he would not embarrass himself with any stray erections back on the trail. He certainly felt played out. Yet it was Veee's whispered words that remained in his fancy. Had he met her on the street in his home town he would not have spared her more than a passing glance, but here on the trail, with their more subtle similarities coming into play, he was falling in love with her. Her non-jealous nature was a factor; she did not begrudge him his incidental passion for Vanja. How many other women would be that tolerant?

They emerged from the water, shook themselves dry, donned clothing, and resumed their march along the trail. Tod was more curious than ever where it was leading them.

It led them straight into a village, the first they had seen here. The inhabitants were human, going about their routine business of gardening, hunting, building, tending children, and trading. They ignored the travelers. That was odd.

"I wonder," Veee said. "Could it be like your village in your home world? Where the people couldn't see me?"

"We'll find out," Tod said. He approached a man who was making a shoe out of leather. "Hello."

"Hello, traveler," the man said. So much for invisibility.

"We have been following the trail. It led us here. Can you tell us anything about it?"

"No." The man smiled. "Let me explain: travelers come for a reason. We do not interfere with them, lest we compromise their mission, but will help if asked. The initiative must come from you; then we can safely respond. In any event we know nothing about your mission, except that it is surely important, as they all are."

"There are many travelers on many missions?"

"Yes, over the years. The centuries. We are all descendants of the folk of prior missions. But yours is the first we have seen here in fifty years. There may have been more recent missions relating to other villages."

"Thank you," Tod said, taken aback. He returned to the others, and relayed what the cobbler had told him. "So it seems we're still on our own."

"Then let's keep following the trail," Vanja said. "Maybe this village is just a way station."

They walked on. The trail led to a small central plaza, wherein a lone man sat on a wooden chair. He was old, with white hair and a white beard, wearing a sparkling robe. Tod saw with surprise that even the man's pupils were almost white. "Hello."

"And you are the task group, arrived at last," the man said, standing. "Welcome. I am the final member of your party. Call me Wizard."

Again Tod was taken aback. "Is that literal?"

"Of course. I have magical powers. Here is a small demonstration." He produced a wand, waved it, and a ravening monster appeared in the air above him. "Illusion," Wizard said. "Because that is the cheapest magic. I can also do telekinesis, but that requires much energy and I prefer not to waste it on a mere demonstration." The monster faded.

"I am Tod Timmins, of Earth," Tod said. "This is Veee, from a more primitive culture. And Bem, nonhuman. And Vanja, a vampire. Do you know anything about why we were summoned here, and what our mission might be?"

"I know only generalities, but those should suffice for the moment. Before we address the subject of our mission, please allow me to scry each of you in turn, to clarify your likely roles."

"Scry?"

"The trail translates accurately, but sometime there is no term in your lexicon to fit the concept. To scry was originally to divine information via a crystal ball. I use it simply to fathom the specifics about a person." He smiled. "It is harmless, merely more cheap magic. I will begin by describing myself. I came to the trail on a mission in my impetuous youth, joined with the other members from divergent realms, and we succeeded in accomplishing our mission in good order. It consisted of rescuing several lives and priceless artifacts from loss when a volcano erupted and spewed molten lava across the escape route. The lava prevented the locals from helping, but our assorted talents sufficed. Then we disbanded, and I returned to my native realm, profiting from the expansion of my perspectives that had occurred here. I had matured especially in judgment and temperament. I was able to handle the uncomfortable situation that had caused me to depart before, and won the girl and the position I coveted, and lived a long and generally satisfying life. But in time my beloved wife died and I became restive. There seemed to be no proper place for me any more. New kinds of magic were coming to the fore that I did not properly understand. I had become a misfit. So when the trail offered again, I took it, of course. It is a signal honor to be chosen, and an extreme rarity for it to happen a second time. And here I am."

"How long ago was this prior mission?" Vanja asked.

"Approximately a thousand years ago, in my frame. But of course time is largely meaningless here."

"You're a thousand years old?" Veee asked, astonished.

Wizard smiled. "You flatter me by suggesting that I do not look my age. Our clan is long-lived, and of course I employed life-extending potions. But it is true that I am approaching the end of my life. This mission should be a fine way to conclude it." He focused on her. "May I scry you first? I assure you the process is physically painless."

"It is painful in some other respect?"

"It can be emotionally, depending on a person's expectations."

"I have no expectations."

"Then the scrying should be painless."

"Do it," she agreed. Tod suspected that she did not believe all of what Wizard said, so was in effect challenging him to prove it. That had perhaps backfired when she did it with Vanja.

Wizard put on a pointed cap painted with stars. The odd thing was that the stars seemed to move slowly across the surface, as if this was not a cap so much as a window to the universe. He took her hand. He focused intently on her. "Interesting. You are from the modern human line as it emerged from Africa to Asia Minor, before it spread to the rest of the world."

"But that's fifty thousand years ago!" Tod protested.

"Indeed, by your evident reckoning. The trail reaches wherever it needs to, to summon relevant individuals." He returned his focus to Veee. "You departed your realm because your skills were not appreciated there. You are a virtual genius of general comprehension, probably the outstanding example of your age." He smiled. "However, the human population was small then, perhaps no more than five thousand individuals. The relatively ignorant men of your society had no comprehension, of course, but even so were wary of your potential. Thus you became a tacit outcast, even before the trap you fell into. They were watching you, alert for just such a pretext. Nubile but untaken women were frowned on, partly because they were considered fair game for the prurient interests of any men in the vicinity. Especially when the woman was as physically well-endowed as you, and able to carry solid loads considerable distances. The other women were not satisfied with that sexual bondage, any more than you were. Later cultures would think of it as institutionalized rape. That mutual disaffection made you eligible for the trail."

Veee stared at him, open-mouthed. "I am just a woman."

"Ah, that's the problem. Your culture does not value women for their intellectual or artistic qualities, only their breeding qualities.

Yours are evidently good, but still your mind overshadowed them, and you were not taken."

Tod saw that the Wizard had scored. Veee was a lot more woman than showed at first glance.

"I have not been bred," Veee protested after a moment.

"Correction: you were bred, but employed a home-made contraceptive douche to ensure that no pregnancy followed."

Veee looked as if he had struck her. Evidently he had scored again. It seemed that she had after all had an expectation: that he would not fathom her most private secrets.

"And here on the trail you have at last discovered the compatibility and love you longed for," Wizard concluded. "Though perhaps not precisely as you might have anticipated."

"You know all this only from your scrying?" Vanja asked, daunted.

"It is simple magic. The immediate facts of a person's situation are present in the mind, easy to fathom."

"You're a mind reader?" Tod asked.

"No. I fathomed her longing because it is part of her situation, not a specific thought. Her private mind is not open to scrying. No one's mind is."

"So you can ascertain a person's general background and situation, and guess at his thoughts or feelings about it," Veee said.

"Exactly, Veee. You understand perfectly, as you should."

"You have answers for us?" Vanja asked. "Such as exactly what we're doing here, apart from surviving?"

"Some. First I need to ascertain what we have here. He looked at Tod. "May I scry you next?"

"Why not." Tod took Veee's place before Wizard.

Wizard focused disconcertingly on him. He took Tod's hand. "You are from a rather more recent frame, where technology is largely triumphant. Machines greatly facilitate most human physical and intellectual exercises. You have no serious social commitments. Women are not generally impressed with you. Yet you have an intellect considerably beyond the norm. You exercise this mainly by playing games. There is one wherein differently shaped pieces, with different rules of motion, move on a flat board marked by colored squares."

"Chess."

"Chess, thank you. You are an excellent player, but hide your ability, because others tend to resent it and you prefer friendship to victory. So you play privately against a machine, with extraordinary skill."

"An Internet chess program that can be set to different levels," Tod said. "The machine doesn't care whether I win or lose; it simply plays an almost perfect game. I lose more than I win, even though I sometimes take hours pondering a single move. I would do worse if I were on the clock." He glanced at the others, who seemed perplexed. "In competition the moves are timed. I'm not a competitor."

"But you set it at the highest level," Wizard said. "Impressive master."

"Grandmaster," Tod said with half a smile.

"If that means what I think it means," Vanja said, "You are a genius player."

Tod shrugged. "I'd probably go to pieces in actual competition. I just play for the challenge."

"And there is the likely reason you were summoned," Wizard said. "Your mental skill in organizing and completing a challenging task. You are the leader."

"But I'm not a leader!" Tod protested. "I'm just an anonymous warehouseman."

"In your home frame," Wizard said. "Not on the trail."

"I'm no leader here either."

"Not by choice."

"But—" He looked desperately at Veee, Vanja, and Bem, but none of them looked supportive.

"You are as reluctant to recognize your role as Veee was to recognize hers," Wizard said. "But for this purpose you must conform."

"I think he means that I can figure out the nature of a situation," Veee said. "But you are the one who organizes it to accomplish the requirement. To get the job done. I tell you the rules; you play the game. Our talents complement each other."

"Exactly," Wizard agreed. "I see that when predators attacked, you were the one who organized resistance and enabled your party to escape."

"He sure did," Vanja said. "I thought we were dead meat in the water, but he set the wolves against the shocks and got us through."

"I did what I had to do," Tod said, embarrassed.

"Exactly," Wizard repeated. He glanced at Vanja. "May I scry you next? I can see without scrying that you hail from an alternate reality. This trail is casting an unusually wide net, if that is not too much of a mixing of terms."

"Will you tell us what you know of our reason for being here?"

"That can not be properly answered until I know more about you."

"You're avoiding the issue."

"The issue is more complicated than you perhaps appreciate. But I will tell you what I can when I have better information."

"Oh, pooh!" Tod had the impression she would normally have used a more vulgar term, but was moderating her speech in line with her decision to befriend the others.

Tod stepped back and the vampire came forward. "If you embarrass me in front of my friends, I'll bite you and make you my love slave," she said with a limited smile as she proffered her hand.

Wizard smiled back. "Don't flirt with me, vamp. I am too old to respond to your wiles, much as I might have liked to in my prime." He focused, and whistled. "Oh, how I would have liked to, you naughty creature! You seduced Tod in public in minutes and made him forget." He frowned. "Yet you failed to complete your conquest, though you could readily have done so. That is not like your kind."

"Can you tell me why?" Vanja asked evenly. She was testing him, as Veee had.

"Because you desire true friendship more than sex or blood, and found a woman capable and worthy of it. Whose friendship you would have forfeited had you absconded with her man." He glanced at Veee. "Smart decision. Instead of fracturing the forming team, you acted to bind it together. I am impressed."

"We vamps are a practical breed."

"You left your home setting because the chief took another woman instead of you. She was barely the shadow of you. Neither as pretty nor as smart, a relatively unskilled dancer, and not nearly as motivated. You were disgusted."

"Right on. Why did he take her?"

"Because not only were you better than she was, you were better than he was. Few men want to marry a woman who is obviously smarter than they are, or even have her for a mistress."

Vanja clapped a hand to her forehead. "*That's right!* How could I not have realized?"

"You were blinded by rage. But your decision was good. He was not worthy of you, and you would have been fed up with him before long. Tod here is much more your type, even if you have to share him."

"You are scoring, Wizard. Why did the trail come for me?"

"You are single minded, too. You clearly possess abilities or traits that are in demand for this mission, though I don't know what they are. Selections can be devious." Wizard turned to Bem. "Will you be scried next?"

Vanja stepped back, impressed as Veee and Tod had been. Bem glided forward, extending an extruded arm. Wizard took it and focused.

And reacted with surprise. "You are no common frustrated entity! You are a prince, or the equivalent!"

"Not here on the trail." But the others were surprised too. Bem had said nothing about this.

"You are destined to inherit what I term for lack of a better description the throne of Snalliverti and assume enormous power," Wizard continued. "Yet you took the trail instead." He focused further. "Ah. Because you felt unworthy. That you would botch the job and disappoint your people. So when the trail beckoned, you took it, leaving your destiny behind." He looked up. "But you are not unworthy, and you must not leave it behind. Your people need you. You will not disappoint them. You are far more qualified than you choose to believe, and you will have motive to succeed. When you are done here you will return."

Bem flashed rebelliously. "This is not my intention."

"Not your present intention. That will change."

"You can scry the future?"

"No. But I can see enough in the present to know the currents channeling you. You will become satisfied that you need to return, as I did my first time."

"Perhaps," Bem said noncommittally.

But Tod believed Wizard, who had identified Bem in a manner

they had not known about. Wizard was authentic.

"Something we have figured out, that maybe you can confirm," Tod said. "We conclude that we are ultimately unified by the arts we privately practice: music, painting, dance, architecture. Does this make sense to you?"

"Perfect sense," Wizard agreed. "You are widely divergent entities who might have trouble getting along together, even on the conducive trail. But your shared artistic creativity gives you a common bond. That is no coincidence."

"Just so," Tod agreed. He knew the others understood what he was doing. "So do you also have an art?"

Wizard smiled. "That was clever of you to fathom. Yes, I share this secret. I do not practice it in my normal frame, but I long to."

He was reticent about it, as they were. He had to be prodded. "And what is that art?"

"I long to be a story teller. Not necessarily an excellent one, merely good enough to hold a small audience, at least for a while."

"Why didn't you do it?"

"Because I am a wizard. It is my duty to perform magic, not to talk about it."

The others nodded.

"I will listen raptly to your stories if you will watch me dance without yawning," Vanja said. "The same goes for the others with their arts."

"Gladly!"

Vanja glanced around, meeting the gaze of each of the others in turn, verifying their approval. Wizard was indeed one of them. "Then welcome to the club."

"I thank you for that welcome," Wizard said sincerely. "It is the kind of acceptance I have longed for all my life."

But that was only the beginning. "Now it is time for you to tell us what else you know," Tod said firmly.

Wizard nodded. "It is time to tell you about the Amoeba."

The members of the group stared at him. What was this? They knew nothing about any amoeba.

Yet.

CHAPTER 5: AMOEBA

"The Amoeba extends across space, time, and alternate realities," Wizard said. "Extending pseudopods where they are needed. It is subtle, avoiding notoriety; few even know of it. But it is a vital force dealing with particular problems, and I think our universe would not survive without it."

"What has this to do with us?" Vanja asked impatiently.

"Patience, vamp, and it will come clear in due course. When there is a problem, the Amoeba assesses it in its fashion and summons individuals to form a team to handle that problem. The Amoeba is not intelligent in the manner we are; it is more like water seeking its own level, or a plant seeking necessary earth, water, and sunlight so it can survive. But it is very sure in its actions, and is always correct in its assessments even if that does not necessarily seem so at first."

"Are you saying that this—this obscure thing is what summoned us here?" Tod asked. "To deal with some problem only it is aware of?"

"Exactly. We owe our presence here, and our ability to survive comfortably here, and to intercommunicate, to the Amoeba. Without it we would be completely ignorant."

"Perhaps we should meet the Amoeba," Bem said. "And ascertain what problem it thinks we can handle."

"You have already met it."

The four looked blankly at Wizard. "I don't remember that meeting," Vanja said.

"The trail!" Veee exclaimed.

Wizard nodded. "And of course you are the first to catch on, Veee. Yes, the extending pseudopods are the sections of the trail, reaching out to our several worlds and conducting us in to the larger body of it. We are inside the Amoeba, and owe our present comfort entirely to its supportive ambiance. In fact—"

There was a scream. They looked, seeing a child caught by an orange scuttling crablike thing, being rapidly carried away. Several villagers were in pursuit, but the crab was outdistancing them.

Tod drew his pistol and fired. He knew he hit the crab, but the bullet had no effect. "Uh-oh," he murmured.

Vanja transformed and flew to intercept it. She landed in front of it, returned to human form, grabbed at it, and put her face to its body. She was biting it.

The crab scuttled a few steps farther, slowed, then settled in place. The villagers caught up and took the crying girl. "Appreciation, miss!" a man called. "You saved her!"

Tod, Veee, and Bem arrived on the scene. The crab had six legs below with single hoof-like claws, six arms above with single knife-like nails, but no sign of eyes or ears, mouth or anus. Now Tod saw the bullet hole through the center of the crab. He had scored, but not killed it. It had taken Vanja's vampire bite to stop it.

A woman, evidently the child's mother, rushed in to pick up the girl. There was blood on her arms and body where the thing's spikes had penetrated, but it looked as though she would survive.

"What is this thing?" Tod asked as they came up to it.

"I believe I know," Bem said. "That also answers why I was summoned here. I have seen this type of thing before, and it is dangerous. We had a ferociously awful time extirpating their invasion before they extirpated us. That is a variety of android. A semi-living creature made in a laboratory or the equivalent, having no mind of its own, to bones, organs, or circulatory system. Animate plastic with light and sound-sensitive skin. All androids connect mentally to the central brain, and are extensions of it; what one knows, all know, instantly. The units feel no pain, physical or emotional and are fearless. The only way to disable them is to cut off their limbs, or melt them in a fire or with acid, or as Vanja demonstrated, inject paralyzing poison to nullify their animation, though I am surprised that worked considering their bloodless nature."

"Our poison spreads by contagion through flesh, needing no blood," Vanja said. "We don't like to pollute what we drink."

"That last is hardly practical on the larger scale," Bem said. "The only reason she got a bite was because it was alone and its limbs were occupied supporting the child. They do defend themselves when attacked, coordinated by the central mind. There will be many more appearing soon, now that this village has been discovered."

"This one relayed what it saw to its brain?" Veee asked.

"Yes. Contact is continuous. So the only reason we have not seen more androids yet must be because this is as yet early in their cycle and not many are available. That will soon change." Bem angled its knob toward the crab. "De-limb it now; it is recovering."

Tod drew his hunting knife and attacked the stirring android. Its upper limbs lifted to fend him off, but he sliced forcefully at each. The blade cut through the tough hide; several strokes were required for each arm, but soon all six mere lying on the ground around it. The android tried to scuttle away, but Vanja caught its hindmost legs to hold it back, while Tod hacked at them. It still tried to run on four, but Vanja caught two more and Tod severed them. Finally it was completely de-limbed and helpless. There was no blood; the cuts were dry, as if the thing really were made of plastic.

"It may still be observing us," Bem said. "Its surface is light sensitive."

"Allow me," Wizard said. He brought out his wand, oriented it, and a jet of flame shot out, bathing the hulk of the android. The substance crackled and scorched, then caught fire as the jet continued. Foul-smelling smoke rose up, making them cough, stinging Tod's eyes. The mound of it reluctantly shrank. This, again, was like burning plastic, Tod thought. Not something they wanted to do often.

The jet stopped. "I think that has ended any perceptive ability it has," Wizard said. "No sense wasting power. It should rot in time and become fertilizer for the local plants."

"What was it going to do with the child?" Vanja asked.

"Carry her back to its brain," Bem said, "which will likely be a pool of protoplasm in a depression, and dump her in. Her body would rapidly dissolve and become more protoplasm, available to make more androids. This is how it expands. All the villagers will be at risk. The android will not stop until all available protoplasm has been consumed. Then it will move on to another village. The longer it continues, the harder it will be to stop. We must not delay our action long."

"What action?" Tod asked, sheathing his knife.

"We must destroy the pool. That will be difficult, because it will be most fiercely defended, even at the outset."

"How can it be destroyed?"

"That is a challenge. It could be burned, if there were fire enough. Possibly cutting all the trees and building a huge bonfire over it would suffice. We managed in our frame to build a large lens and cause a focus ray of our star to burn it up, but there is no sufficient technology here."

"I believe that will be my job," Wizard said. "I will magically bomb it. Such a bomb will destroy its animation, leaving inert substance. But that course is fraught with its own complications. This is evidently the mission for which we were summoned; we must organize our campaign." He looked at Tod. "Take over, leader."

Tod realized that he had no choice. He surprised himself by taking hold. "We will need to organize the villagers, as they are most at risk. They need to build temporary fortifications to stop the androids. You can do that, Bem, as you know the nature of the attack that will soon come. We must also locate the android pool and discover an avenue to reach it—one it will not be aware of, for the sake of surprise. That's your job, Vanja, in bat form. Try not to let them see you."

"They know I can transform, because this thing saw me."

"But they don't yet know that we know their nature," Veee said. "They won't expect us to spy on them."

"Got it," Vanja agreed.

"And we must figure out how our several abilities will contribute most effectively to this campaign. You can do that, Veee. Meanwhile I need to know more about the Amoeba, in case there is relevant information that will facilitate our mission, or indeed, make it possible to accomplish." He paused momentarily. "Get on it, Bem and Vanja; you know better than I do what to do. Veee, stay with me and learn what you can; you will define the rules of this game. Wizard—let's go somewhere private and talk."

"I am impressed," Bem said, flashing. It slid toward the center of the village, issuing a siren-like call for attention. The villagers began gathering around it, having seen the danger to the child. They had evidently encountered alien creatures before, so knew that they were not necessarily enemies. Bem was a good alien.

"I am impressed too," Vanja said. She transformed and flew away. The villagers now knew that she, too, was on their side.

Veee merely squeezed his hand.

Wizard led the way along the trail through the village, coming to a covered spring surrounded by a low wall. They sat on the wall. "What else is there about the Amoeba?" Tod asked. "You had told us that we are in its ambiance, when we were interrupted by the android."

"And I would like to know how it is that you have not suffered sickness here," Veee said. "Have you not eaten anything?"

"I have eaten, but suffered only a marginal queasiness. That is because this is not my first venture here. I was quite ill the first time. That is an aspect of it: travelers become integrated as they ingest substance within the Amoeba. At that point they have aspects of it outside and inside them. That normally causes their bodies to react, but thereafter they are acclimatized and have no further trouble of that nature."

"What about the predators on the trail?" Tod asked. "Was that a challenge to test our fitness to survive?"

"I think not. I suspect that predators are invasive species that have learned that where there are trails, there are travelers, and those are prey. So they close in on targets of opportunity. The Amoeba does not act directly, so can't stop them. But quite possibly it selects creatures who are capable of dealing with incidental predators; that would be part of their qualifications for the mission."

"And the trail that ended in a box canyon?" Veee asked.

"Bem can climb. He enabled you to make that ascent. The team as a whole can do things that its individual components can't. The Amoeba would not consciously plan that, but would simply know that you could handle that problem."

Tod nodded. So it did make sense. Still, he had questions. "I think you said that the Amoeba is not intelligent. How can it reason out exactly what will be needed?"

"I have wondered that myself. I have concluded that it can fathom, if not the future, at least the probability of success. It summons the creatures that maximize that probability. It may not know what their individual qualifications are, merely that the team as a whole has a reasonable chance."

"Still, it selects individuals," Veee said.

"Again, this is my conclusion, not my knowledge. I am unable to scry the Amoeba. But I think that it sends pseudopods out to intercept individuals who will contribute to the essential whole. It may be that when it finds one, it modifies its search for the next, so as neither to duplicate abilities or miss any. So when you entered the trail, Tod, that further defined the need for the next." Wizard smiled. "It must have been quite a challenge, if it had to reach fifty thousand years into your past to find her."

"That's another thing," Tod said. "The Amoeba can reach across time, to bring Veee here, and space to bring Bem?"

"And alternate universes, to bring Vanja and myself," Wizard agreed. "Because magic is not effective in your realm, but seems to be necessary for this mission."

"And in the ambiance of the Amoeba, it seems that both science and magic work," Tod said. "And whatever alien abilities Bem has."

"And we can talk to each other," Veee said. "When we left the trail, we could not. In fact, I did not really exist in Tod's world."

"The Amoeba is a marvelous entity," Wizard said. "It not only brings in divergent creatures, wherever they may be, it enables them to survive comfortably in a common environment, and to interact compatibly. You would not survive long on Bem's planet if you could go there; its air is not breathable, and its gravity is twice yours. But within the Amoeba neither of you are even aware of such things. In this manner it enables a truly remarkable mix of creatures."

Tod smiled. "I call it the trail mix."

"Apt description."

"Yet the Amoeba can't simply solve its problems directly?" Tod asked. "Without going to the considerable trouble of bringing in, as you put it, divergent entities and making them comfortable?"

"The Amoeba, as I understand it, can take no direct physical or mental action. For that it depends on us. Each time a crisis arises, it summons appropriate creatures to handle it, then lets them go or stay, as they prefer. The villagers are descendants of the members of prior missions, reverted to a comfortable state where the climate is equitable and food readily available. Elsewhere there are surely villages of vampires and of bems, too. But they lack the skills necessary to handle the current crisis, which is why we were summoned."

Tod nodded. "When you make life too easy, people relax into indolence. I've seen it on Earth. It's a wonder the villagers aren't fat."

"The Amoeba takes care of that too!" Veee said, catching on. "It keeps them healthy regardless!"

"It is truly a paradise," Wizard agreed. "That seems to be the reward for accomplishing its purposes: an ideal retirement."

"Don't they get bored?" Tod asked.

"While I waited for your arrival, I observed the activities of the villagers. They played many games and had much sex, seeming not concerned that I was observing." He smiled. "Vanja will like them."

"I saw some children, but not many," Veee said.

"Population seems to be constant," Wizard said. "When a villager ages and dies, a child is conceived and born. There seems to be no venereal disease. They accept that as the natural order."

"The women have nothing to lose except boredom," Veee said. "That must make them amenable."

Tod glanced at her. "And you are not?"

"I must pace Vanja, lest I lose you," she said seriously. "Otherwise I would be more reticent. However, now that I know there will be no baby, I am free to enjoy it. If we were to retire here, I would not disappoint you."

"Free sex," Tod said. "Much as I like the notion, I'm not sure I would settle for that."

"Which is perhaps why the option of going home exists," Wizard said. "Those who are wary of Paradise are free to leave it."

"You will go home and leave me, Tod?" Veee's tone and expression were dangerously neutral.

"No! I don't think I could leave you, Veee. I think I love you, and have a passion for Vanja. But settling into sloth, with no physical or mental or social challenge—that's not for me either."

She smiled. "Vanja is adventurous too. I would rather share you with her than lose you."

"Maybe we can travel. Who knows where the trails of the Amoeba will take us?"

"Anywhere in space, time, or alternate reality," Wizard said. "Paradise is not limited to sloth."

Still, Tod was not quite satisfied. "The benefits the Amoeba provides seem marvelous. Yet I can't be sure it really exists. It could be simply a magical path."

"Yes," Veee agreed. "It is like a god."

"I can't say I believe in any god," Tod said. "I mean, some invisible, intangible entity that watches over us all without interfering? What is the point?"

"There could be nothing," Veee agreed.

"Skepticism is healthy," Wizard said. "I was a skeptic too. But I came to believe."

"What convinced you?" Tod asked.

"A subtle thing. While the Amoeba is not intelligent or even conscious, as far as I can tell, it does know what's in a person's mind. It has to, to choose the right people for the job at hand. I learned to sense its tuning in. When there is anything odd or incomplete, it orients on it, as if to verify that the person is correct for the team. It's just a momentary focus, not an action."

"How does that prove the existence of the Amoeba?" Tod asked.

"Perhaps we can demonstrate. I can't read minds, I can only feel the Amoeba when it orients. That should be enough."

"I am in doubt also," Veee said.

"Try to think of something that bothers you, both of you," Wizard said. "When I feel the Amoeba respond, I will speak, and then you can tell me what you were thinking of."

"That does not seem like much of a test," Tod said.

"Try it and see."

Tod and Veee pondered. What came to his mind seemed totally irrelevant. He was about to pass over it, when Wizard spoke. "Now. What is in your mind?"

"It's just a schoolyard ditty I don't get," Tod said. "Nothing important."

"Describe it."

"A poem, actually. But everyone else laughed as though it was dirty. It seemed innocent to me. I shut up because I didn't want to be ridiculed for being stupid. I never mentioned it to anyone."

"Recite it now."

Tod was embarrassed, but plowed ahead. "Oh Nellie Priss went out to pick some flowers," he recited. "She stood in grass up to her ankle tops. She went to the coop to let out a poor little chicken, and now she sits and shivers in the moonlight." He spread his hands. "It doesn't even rhyme."

Veee was evidently trying to keep a straight face. "I almost heard something else," she said. "Something that did rhyme. Maybe the rendering into my language erred."

"Say what you almost heard," Wizard said.

"It is not nice. I am ashamed of my wicked imagination."

"Say it," Tod growled impatiently.

"Oh Nellie Priss went out to piss," she said. "She stood in grass up to her ass. She went to the coop to let out a poop, and now she sits and shits."

Suddenly Tod got it. "Oh my god! Now I remember how they stressed some of the words. She went to the coop to let out a po-oo—or little chicken. How could I have missed it!"

"You had a conservative upbringing," Wizard said. "You tuned out the dirtiness. That rendered it pointless."

"And the Amoeba sensed my distress over it," Tod said.

"Exactly. You may not consider that proof of the Amoeba's existence."

"No, I think now I do, crazy as it seems."

"Let me continue," Veee said.

They waited while she pondered.

"Now," Wizard said suddenly.

"Oh, I don't think—"

"The Amoeba knows. Tell us."

"But it might annoy Tod."

Tod smiled. "Which is why you prefer to avoid it. I appreciate your courtesy, and promise not to be annoyed."

She considered momentarily, then took a breath. "It's that we have lore about pretend people who look and talk and act like real ones, but are really zombies or spooks who will kill you if you trust them. They—they can even have sex, and you can't know the difference. But if you then sleep in their arms, they will throttle you. It bothers me. If I encountered such a creature, how could I know? I don't want to run away from a real man I like." She paused. "I—I think that when I first met Tod, I feared he could be such a thing. He seemed real, but he was different. It took me time to trust him."

Which further explained her initial reticence. "You feared I could be a robot. A machine that seemed like a man, but was not alive."

"Yes," she said faintly. "Can you forgive me?"

"There's nothing to forgive! You had a sensible concern, considering your culture. And I am curious too: if you were a robot, capable of emulating a live human being even to the extent of having sex, how could I know? How could I risk sleeping in your embrace?"

"You trusted me."

"Maybe I was more foolish than you were, because I never doubted you, and I should have."

"When you slept in my arms, I knew you were real." She smiled. "You even snored."

"It remains a good question: how could either of us be sure before risking sleeping that the other was real and not a robot, zombie, changeling, or simply an assassin?"

"Yes. I knew I could not ask, because a false person would lie, saying he was real."

"I wonder," Tod said, getting an idea. "A fake would never admit to being fake, would he? Because that would ruin his mission. So you can be sure of his answer."

"Yes. So I didn't ask."

"But you see, that may be the key. Suppose you require him to play the game of reversal: to say the exact opposite of what he means. Then you ask him point blank: are you real?"

Her brow furrowed. "But he would say no, meaning yes."

"Would he? A genuine human being is sophisticated enough to lie by indirection, but a simple fake who exists only to kill a person is unlikely to have that capacity. Chances are he can't say no, because that seems like a confession that will damn him. So all he can say is yes, or nothing. Either dooms him."

Veee looked at Wizard. "Does this make sense?"

"Yes," Wizard said. "No facsimile is as complicated mentally as a live person. Otherwise he would become a person in his own right, and seek to join, not kill you."

She smiled. "Let's play that game a moment, Tod. To say the opposite."

She had something in mind. "Okay."

"I hate you."

"I hate you too."

She moved into him and kissed him ardently. "You are real!"

He squeezed her bottom. "So are you." It seemed there had been a lingering doubt in her mind that this negated.

"Is your doubt about the Amoeba similarly resolved?" Wizard asked.

Veee paused as she disengaged. "Yes. I don't know why."

"I don't know why either," Tod said. "Now that I consider it, this may clarify our identities as real people, but the Amoeba could still not exist. Logically I know that, yet I accept the Amoeba."

"And there is the proof," Wizard said. "The Amoeba identified your concerns, allowed you to work them out, and then caused you to accept the Amoeba itself as you accept each other. It is similar to the way the Amoeba causes the disparate members of the team to get along together, to like each other, despite being so different or even natural enemies. It is that touch in your mind, that you know is not your own logic, that authenticates it."

Both Tod and Veee pondered that. Did it really make sense? "Let's kiss again," he said.

She smiled and kissed him again. That would have to do.

But they had other business to handle. Tod focused on the present. "Now all we have to do is get rid of the androids before they get rid of us, and then the Amoeba itself."

"Exactly," Wizard agreed. "I will cooperate to the best of my abilities, which are considerable, but I am no thinker or leader. You must formulate the plan and put it into action."

"No thinker? You just explained how the Amoeba persuaded us to believe in it."

"My insight is based on prior experience. I have had an intervening lifetime to reflect on such nuances. You must take charge."

"I will do my best," Tod said wryly.

"That may not be enough," Veee said.

The two men looked at her. "My best will not suffice?" Tod asked.

"As I now understand the Amoeba, the best of one person is never enough. It requires the best of every member of the team, and of the team itself."

"Yes, of course," Tod agreed, vaguely nettled. "I meant merely that I will do my part."

She smiled at him. "What I really meant is that getting rid of the android pool won't be enough. Probably the villagers could do that themselves, now that they have been alerted. Our team must have been assembled for a larger purpose. One that requires more of us than merely dealing with the present menace."

Tod exchanged a glance with Wizard. "There is a larger menace?"

"I think of it as like an infection, a disease that troubles the Amoeba itself. If the androids consume all the villagers and go on to other villages, in time there will not be any people or animals or perhaps plants left. The Amoeba will become a desert, unable to support any new recruits."

"Maybe a better analogy is cancer," Tod said. "A tumor forms and grows, leeching off the body of the host, even requiring it grow blood vessels to supply the cancer itself. Then it metastasizes, or colonizes other parts of the body. That spread is what will likely kill the host."

"Cancer," Veee agreed, though the term was evidently new to her. "The android pool will seed other pools. These must be stopped. But I am thinking of the pool that seeded this one. Where is it? That is the one we must locate and abolish. Otherwise we will simply be fighting the daughter pools endlessly."

Wizard nodded. "You have a point. We are dealing with an effect rather than a cause. We must handle the effect, then go after the cause, wherever it may be."

"That could be a daughter pool itself," Tod said. "There could be a chain of them. But I think not a long chain, because if the problem had appeared long ago, we or some other team would have been summoned to deal with it then. So probably this is the first one. Still, it had to come from somewhere."

"A single orange crab," Wizard said. "Scuttling through the reaches of the Amoeba, until it finds a suitable place to pool. It did not invent itself; it has to have come from somewhere else. Somewhere outside the Amoeba."

"Where we can't go," Veee said.

"It came down a trail, down a pseudopod, as we did," Tod said. "We must find that trail and close it off."

Wizard shook his head. "Trails can't be closed by others. Each trail remains open as long as its person remains in the Amoeba. That's so any participant can always go home. Few do, but that option remains until they die."

"I don't want to kill anyone," Tod said quickly.

"This merely acquaints you with the parameters of the challenge."

Tod sighed. "I am coming to appreciate them. Now we should help the others get organized."

They returned to the village. The men were building a rampart by digging a trench and piling the dirt into a low wall. The women were gathering firewood and forming it into a kind of wall outside the rampart. The children were collecting berries and storing them in baskets, food for a likely siege. Bem was clearly organizing them well. But would it suffice? It depended on how many androids came how soon.

Bem spied them and glided toward them. "The villagers appreciate the danger," it said. "But I am uncertain they have the resources to abate a larger attack of this nature. The supply of wood is limited, and it will not be easy to battle the androids when they come in an organized mass."

"We'll have to help them," Tod said. "If we can figure out how best to do it."

The bat flew in, transforming as she landed. "I located the pool,"

Vanja said. "It's in a mountain crevice, barely accessible to two legged creatures. We will have a problem reaching it, especially if we need to be unobserved."

"How far advanced is the pool?" Bem asked.

"Hard to tell. Depends how much volume is hidden in that crevice. There are maybe a dozen androids bringing in small animals and dumping them in. They scream as they dissolve."

"What about plants?"

"No plants being dumped. Is that significant?"

"Yes," Bem said. "The androids that attacked our realm were omnivorous. They consumed plants as well as animals. This may be a more limited variant."

"Too bad they are not limited to plant life," Veee said.

"Probably plant fiber is harder to digest," Tod said. "They are going for the easy stuff first."

"So what's the plan?" Vanja asked.

"Is an attack on the village likely today or tonight?"

"I think not. They are still foraging for animals."

"Could we attack the pool today?"

"I can show you where it is, but I think we'll need to wipe out the loose androids before we get near the pool."

Tod considered. "I think the best way to wipe them out is to wait for their attack on the village. If they are largely mindless, we can chop them up, then attack the pool immediately while its defenses are depleted. Meanwhile we can help the villagers prepare."

They did that, helping with digging, gathering, and organization of defensive units. "You saw how that orange crab ran off with the child," Tod told the villagers. "There will be more of them, maybe larger, and they'll try to haul away adults too. The fires should balk them, but some will get by, and those ones need to be chopped immediately."

As the day ended without an attack, they posted watches and settled down for the night. "We don't know when they'll attack," Tod said. "Just that they will. We must be sure to know it the moment they do. Meanwhile, eat, rest, sleep. It may be a long siege, once it starts."

The villagers retired, and the team settled in the forest between the village and the distant pool. "I will post a magic alert," Wizard said. "That's cheap magic, and it will warn us in plenty of time to set up for combat."

"We have a small tent," Tod told Wizard. "Maybe you should use it to sleep."

"That's generous, but I have no need." Wizard moved his hands in a weaving manner, and a small dome of light formed. He walked into it and lay down, and it covered him like a protective bubble, which it surely was.

"Then if you girls wish to share the tent?"

"We have been through this before," Vanja said. "Strip and lie down."

"But we should be resting. We can't be sure how long it will be, or when we can rest again."

"Well take it easy on you tonight," Vanja said. "Once each. Then we'll sleep. Good night, Bem."

"Good night," Bem echoed.

Tod stripped and lay down on his back. Vanja lay on top of him, put his hands on her bottom, kissed him, and soon evoked his ardor. She took him in, seeming to climax with him. Then she moved aside and Veee clasped him, not trying for sex, just kissing and holding him. To his surprise she soon nodded off to sleep, and so did he. It was further confirmation of their trust in each other.

But later in the night Veee hauled him onto her and into her, and brought him to a gentle climax. Then she slept again, and he did.

Vanja, beside them, slept through it, or seemed to. Evidently the two women had worked out their turns beforehand. It was very pleasant.

Morning came, and all was quiet. Vanja transformed to bat and flew off to scout the enemy. She reported that the pool was quiet. Even the androids had disappeared. What were they up to?

The day passed without incident. The village was ready for an attack and siege, but none came. Some people were starting to evince impatience. Had their routine been disrupted for nothing?

They spent a second night waiting. This time Veee did Tod first, and Vanja took her turn hours later after he recovered potency. They were managing him carefully. But where were the androids?

"I wonder whether we are being too conservative," Tod said. "Maybe we should raid the pool now, rather than wait for it to act."

"I think that would not be wise," Bem said. "The pool may be trying to provoke us to premature action."

"Just how smart is it?"

"That is difficult to ascertain. It may be programmed to act randomly, so as to catch opposition off-guard. But it will surely act, and have fair impact when it does."

"I wonder."

Then the attack came. Not large androids, but small ones. Thousands of them. They swarmed out of the forest like an orange carpet.

"Light the fire!" Tod cried.

The men lit the fire barrier. But the bugs diverted around it and came on, down into the ditch, up over the rampart. They got on the people, stabbing them with their points. There were screams of pain and horror.

Most of their prepared defenses were useless. The pool might not have a brain, but it had outsmarted them.

"Stomp them," Vanja suggested.

"Stomp them!" Tod cried to the villagers. "With your hardest shoes. Squish them underfoot!"

The men did, but there were far too many bugs to stop this way.

"Burn them with torches," Wizard suggested.

"Burn them with torches!" Tod yelled.

The villagers did, and the acrid smell of burning android flesh suffused the area. But still there were too many.

"Hot water!" Veee said to Tod.

"Hot water!" Tod cried. "Boiling if you have it. Pour it on them? Cook them!"

Women had pots of heated cooking water. The men helped them haul these out, and pour the water on the advancing horde. The bugs collapsed and became inert. They were protoplasm, and could not retain their animation when overheated. Their small size meant that the heat penetrated quickly through their bodies. The water flowed out, catching them in a widening circle before cooling.

It didn't get them all, but now the android horde had been decimated, and stomping was more effective on the remainder. The tide was turning. The villagers were winning.

The surviving bugs retreated. In moments they were gone, uncatchable in the rugged forest. But the battle had been won.

"Thanks to you!" a villager told Tod. "You told us how!"

Tod would have corrected him, because it had been the spot advice of the others that did it, but realized that they wanted to believe in a leader. "It isn't over yet," he warned them. "This was just the first battle."

That night Veee and Vanja nestled close against him from either side. "You were great!" Veee said, kissing his right ear. "Stunning," Vanja agreed, nibbling without biting his left ear.

"I was a figurehead. You know that."

Each put a leg over his thigh, pressed her breasts against his side, and kissed his neck. "Just keep it up," Veee said, rubbing against him. "And hard," Vanja said, catching hold of his member.

"You think I'm good for only one thing," he grumbled.

"Mediocre, but improving," Vanja said, laughing.

This time they actually alternated penetrations, each taking him in and squeezing before quickly withdrawing, until he erupted into one of them. "I win!" Veee said.

"But I was in Vanja," Tod protested.

Veee patted his shoulder. "The bet was who could dip you most often without getting caught."

They had been playing to avoid the climax, like musical chairs. "You girls are incorrigible."

"Well, we love you," Vanja said. "At least I do a little, and she does a lot."

"And I think I love both of you, a little or a lot."

They melted against him.

"Alarm!" Wizard called.

All three scrambled out of the tent, naked, grabbing for knives. There, illuminated by Wizard's magic shield, was a single android the size of a rhinoceros. It was barging toward the village.

"Surprise attack," Bem said. "Both in the timing and the organization. That is more sophisticated than what we encountered before."

"Villagers!" Tod shouted. "Big one attacking! Vacate!"

There was a rustle as the villagers woke and scrambled. Soon they saw the monster. They tried to flee from it, but it outran them and spiked a man from behind. The man was carried along helplessly, if not already dead, surely doomed.

"Oh, damn!" Tod swore.

"The spikes can't reach below," Veee said. "If you get six people to attack the legs—"

"The three of us, and three villagers," Tod said. "Men, here to me! Do as I do!" He ran toward the monster android.

Village men joined him, clearly frightened but desperate. The android paused, searching for new prey. It scuttled toward them.

Tod dived under it and wrapped his arms about one of its trunk-like legs. Vanja followed, catching the leg beside him. Veee caught a third. Three village men caught on, and dived for the remaining legs, clinging tight. The android stood in place, not seeming to understand what was happening.

"Carve!" Tod yelled, unlimbering his large knife. He stabbed at the rubbery flesh. It yielded reluctantly, but he kept at it, making slow progress.

The android ran, hauling them along on its sex legs without managing to dislodge them. They continued to carve, and before long the legs started coming off. The monster collapsed and the people scrambled clear of the stabbing upper limbs. They had incapacitated it, and would be able to destroy it at their leisure. It was another victory.

But obviously the android threat had not been abated. They had won another battle, not the war.

How were they going to save the villagers, themselves, and the Amoeba? It was Tod's job to figure that out, but at this stage he wasn't sure what to do.

CHAPTER 6: ANDROIDS

Tod left the villagers to reduce the android hulk, chopping at its limbs and body with axes and killing it with buckets of boiling water. This took time, and in the reprieve he called a council of war for the team.

"I think the android pool has certain hard-wired reactions," he said. "If one thing is balked, it tries the next on its list, until it finds what works. A single dog-sized bug was stopped, so it tried a swarm of insect sized bugs. When they were stopped, it tried a really massive one. We don't know what it will try next, but I think we can't leave the village until we know it is sufficiently protected. Then we'll go after the pool itself. Are there any suggestions?"

"You're doing fine, lover," Vanja said. "If you crave a spot diversion, I am at your service." Her painted décolletage slid down to expose more white breast, though it was only a color change. Her body was always exposed, technically.

"Thank you, vamp." He did not want to admit that the change

excited him despite his knowledge of its nature. She had the finest figure he had ever seen, and knew it. It never stopped tempting him, despite his thorough familiarity with it. "But what I really want from you at the moment is a plan to save the village, or to attack the android pool."

She inhaled deeply, making her breasts seem to swell out of their illusory harness. "That's easy. Extend the wall around to enclose the village, and set big pots heating water at regular intervals, with people to tend them and watch for attacks. They should be able to hold off a siege, once that's done."

"Veee, what's wrong with that plan?" Tod asked, hoping she would see something he had missed.

"Not enough water," Veee said promptly. "They will need a copious supply, which has to be hauled in by the bucketful from the river a quarter mile away. The haulers will get impaled and carried away to make protoplasm."

She had come through, thanks to her ability to appreciate the essence of a situation. "And how do we deal with that, Bem?"

"Either divert the river to intersect the village, or build the fortress beside or across the river."

"Which is better, Wizard?"

"Easier to move the unbuilt fortress than the established river, which the androids could readily undivert if they thought of it."

"Do they have the wit to think of it, Bem?"

"The pool is a creature of flow that just might understand the principle. Best not to risk it."

"Move the fortress it is," Tod agreed. "Now we tell the natives."

They did. When a villager questioned the harder work, Tod answered with authority. They got to work.

But Tod was unsatisfied. "The more time passes, and the stronger the androids get, the more I think it was a mistake to wait on the enemy. We should have gone after the pool at the outset."

"Bem and Vanja recommended against it," Veee reminded him.

"Yes, and I heeded their advice. But now we know that this pool is different, and probably worse, than what Bem saw or Vanja judged. I think we should raid the pool now. With luck we'll take it out. If not, at least it will be a distraction while the villagers complete their construction."

"I agree," Bem said. "What worked against the pool in my frame seems not to be working here."

"And I am no strategist," Vanja said. "I should have kept my mouth shut."

"No, I want input from all of you," Tod said. "Then I can make decisions based on the best team information. So now we'll raid. I am not used to being a leader; I'm learning as I go. I think the pool won't expect a sudden attack on it, when we've been purely defensive so far, so let's take the most direct route. Our purpose is to get Wizard there so he can bomb the pool. Vanja, lead the way; you know the route."

"Follow me," she said, and set off at a brisk walk.

They followed. "You're watching her behind," Veee murmured.

"You know I am. But I'll watch yours too if you care to join her up front." He patted her bottom. "Especially if you put on that little grass skirt."

She smiled, appreciating his appreciation, knowing it was genuine. "Some other time."

"Soon."

"Soon," she agreed. He knew she liked being courted, rather than being forced and left.

The route led into mountainous terrain, where the path became narrow. "I smell android," Vanja called back. "Be alert."

"I am ready," Wizard said. "However—"

Then the androids pounced. They erupted out of the foliage front, rear, and to either side, half a dozen bear-sized orange crabs, and closed in with spikes stabbing. Vanja transformed and flew up and clear, but the others were caught. "Wizard!" Tod cried.

Light flashed. Then Tod, Bem, and Veee sailed up after Vanja's bat form, floating safely above the androids. But where was Wizard? He had disappeared.

They floated back down the path. The androids, balked, followed, clicking their spikes. Then the floating became flying, and they zoomed ahead and lost the androids behind.

They landed. Wizard reappeared. It seemed that he had made himself undetectable so that the androids could not locate him even when he was among them, and ran back down the path while guiding the floaters. "I have exhausted my power," he said, and collapsed. He had warned them there were limits, which was why he normally used cheap magic, like illusion. He had done what he had to, but seriously depleted himself in the process.

Tod took over. "I'll carry him," he said. "Keep moving so they don't catch up."

"No, I will carry him," Veee said. "You must be free to fight if they come." She bent, heaved Wizard over her shoulder, and walked rapidly downhill.

Tod watched her, amazed. She was solidly constructed, with muscular arms and legs, and had said she could carry well. Now he appreciated how literally she meant that. Wizard was a small man, a relatively light burden, but still this was impressive. "Thank you," he said faintly.

Vanja flew down to land on Tod's shoulder. She was large for a bat, but still small compared to her human form; he had no trouble supporting her. She was facing back, so she could watch the path behind them and alert him the moment anything showed. That meant he could concentrate on moving forward as rapidly as feasible. Bem was gliding rapidly along, having no trouble keeping the pace.

The androids did not catch up. Tod realized that they might not even have pursued the party, either because they didn't realize it had landed, or because prey floating away was not what they were programmed for. Programmed responses had their limits, especially when encountering innovative moves.

They returned to the village. Veee set Wizard down carefully in the little tent. "Bem?" she asked.

Bem formed the blanket shape and spread itself over Wizard.

Vanja took off and flew back, reconnoitering. Soon she returned, transformed, and reported that there was no pursuit; the androids had disappeared.

"Thank you," Tod said. "And thank you, Veee, for the carrying; that was impressive."

She shrugged. "The men of my tribe did not welcome it."

Tod took hold of her, enfolded her, and kissed her. "Maybe you are an acquired taste. I have acquired it." He glanced at Vanja. "And I appreciate your qualities too. You really helped by alerting us."

"We all contribute in the manner the Amoeba must have intended," she said.

"That is surely the case," he agreed. "But it seems your original advice was good: I messed things up."

"None of us were expecting an ambush," Veee said.

"They saw us coming," he said. "Or the pool's program did. It must have had prior experience of that sort. I was thinking the androids were stupid, and they are, but the pool is savvy about this sort of thing. I should have anticipated that." He took a deep breath.

"Now Wizard is out of commission, so we can't try to bomb the pool until he recovers. We'll have to continue our defensive measures for a day or three, depending on how long he takes."

"But he did save us," Veee said. "He is a valuable member of the team."

"He certainly is," Tod agreed. "All of you are."

They returned to work helping the villagers build the fortress.

Something odd happened. A pack of wolfkeys came through, causing the villagers to grab their weapons, but did not attack. Instead they ran on by as if pursued.

"What would make those predators flee?" Tod asked, surprised.

"Androids," Vanja said succinctly.

A wolf-sized android appeared. It too ignored the armed villagers and moved on in evident pursuit of the wolfkeys.

"They are going after the easier prey first," Veee said.

"At least they are showing us some respect," Vanja said.

Then they heard the growling and howling.

"Vanja," Tod said.

She transformed and took off. Soon she was back. "And the androids chased them into a trap," she said. "We represent the back part of it; a larger band of androids is the front part, forming a semicircle. Neat ploy."

"Using us to help complete their enclosure," Tod said. "If that's not intelligence, it's a program to be respected and feared."

"The latter, I think," Bem said.

"But the difference between intelligence and a program," Veee said, "is that we should be able to outsmart the program. Probably it developed to surround and capture prey, and we were here, so it used us, maybe without even realizing that we weren't more androids in the larger scheme."

"We had better hope that's it," Tod said. "Otherwise they may outmaneuver us similarly, when it is our turn to be the prey."

They kept working on the fortress, which was taking shape with reasonable dispatch because the entire village was working hard under Bem's direction.

Then the androids returned. This time it was a pack of about twenty wolf-sized ones, each laden with a wolfkey. They scuttled right past the fort and splashed through the river without pausing. Soon they were gone.

"They must have seen the fortress," Tod said.

"And did not react to it," Veee said.

"Well, they're not intelligent. The pool must have sent them after the wolfkeys and they ignored everything else."

"I don't trust that. The pool may be building up a swarm large enough to overwhelm the fort."

"Maybe," he agreed. "But I doubt it will attack with any particular strategy. If it just sends a huge pack, we should be able to fend it off." But he was uneasy. "Still, maybe you should ponder what else it may try, so we won't be caught entirely by surprise."

"I will," she agreed.

Work on the fortress continued, and it was developing nicely. Meanwhile there was no attack, and the men and women of the village ranged out to forage, always in pairs or larger groups, in case they encountered more androids.

Tod ranged out too, exploring the terrain, accompanied by Veee and Vanja so as to take the same precautions they required of the villagers. The women took turns embracing and kissing him on the fly, not seeking sex, just keeping him warmed up. How could he protest, as long as this did not interfere with their scouting?

They found a glade with patches of colored berries, and paused to pick and eat some.

"Continue picking," Veee murmured. "And look to your left. There is an android watching us." She was always highly aware of her surroundings.

Tod glanced and saw it: an orange crab the size of a rabbit, perched on a boulder, motionless. "Are there others?"

"Yes. But they too seem merely to be observing."

"That's curious. I would have expected them to mindlessly attack. That's why we are in a group, with weapons ready."

"That's why they aren't attacking," Vanja said. "They know we can beat them off and disable them."

"Rather, the pool knows," Veee said. "But they have seen us, and may have been watching us all along. Why aren't they going elsewhere?"

"Hoping we get distracted and become vulnerable?" Tod asked. It was eerie, having the vicious things lurking without making a hostile move. "Like a zombie faking friendliness, until the victim sleeps?"

"Why don't we test it?" Vanja asked. "Veee, guard our backs." She turned to Tod.

"I will," Veee said, continuing her picking and eating, but with her knife ready to draw swiftly. She seemed to be a woman of no jealousy, and he appreciated that about her too.

"What?" Tod asked as Vanja embraced him.

"We're going to seem distracted, to provoke their attack," she said. "Get your pants off."

"But if they do attack—"

"Veee will warn us, and we'll be ready. Keep your knife in your hand." She had her own knife out similarly.

Bemused, he cooperated. With Vanja, almost any pretext would do for sex. He disengaged, dropped his trousers and undershorts, then approached her. She now stood with her back to a tree-trunk, her clothing gone. Despite the tension of the situation, he got an erection. The vampire could arouse him any time she wanted, and loved proving it.

They embraced, each holding a naked blade as if about to stab the other. The androids did not attack.

"Get it in," Vanja whispered, watching past his shoulder.

"But if they attack at that moment—"

"Then pull out and whirl, even if you have to spill on the ground. This is more business than pleasure." She looked again. "One is coming closer."

This was unusual sex, even for the vampire. He bent his knees, oriented, and entered her. He waited, but there was still no attack.

"It seems to be trying to get the best view," Vanja said. "Well, android, what do you make of this?" She moved her belly against him while turning slightly outward, so that the connection of their bodies was visible. What a show-off!

"Maybe they are fans of pornography," Tod said, not entirely facetiously.

"It is certainly looking." She clenched her vagina, and that brought on his climax. He thrust repeatedly, ejaculating, trusting her to alert him when the attack came.

"They're going," Veee announced.

"They must be prudish," Tod gasped as he ebbed.

"I wonder," Vanja said. "I thought they were waiting for our inattention, but it seems they or the pool really were interested in what men do with women. Once they saw that, they moved on to other things. The pool has learned what it sought."

"If they come again, my turn," Veee said.

"Why should the pool have any interest in sex?" Tod asked as he cleaned up and put his trousers back on. "Bem says the androids are completely asexual. They reproduce by being made, not by breeding."

"That is the mystery," Vanja agreed.

"I don't like mysteries when the enemy is this dangerous," Tod said. "I think we'd better fathom what it's up to. The individual androids may be mindless, but the pool has what amounts to dangerous cunning."

"I will think about it," Veee said.

They moved on, but saw no more androids. The mystery remained.

Nothing further occurred that day. The fortress was nearing completion. When would the attack come?

They consulted with Wizard and Bem in the evening. Wizard had recovered enough to talk, but remained physically depleted. "I apologize for becoming a burden."

"No burden!" Tod and Veee said almost together.

"This is indeed odd," Bem said. "The ones we dealt with attacked, retreated, or bided their time. They did not observe. That suggests a more devious pool entity. They should not care at all about prey interactions of any nature."

"That was our thought," Tod said. "We fear that we will not like the resolution of this mystery."

"If only we could have taken out the pool early," Vanja said. "Had I spotted that defense force in time..."

"It was hiding," Veee said. "They knew we would try. It was an ambush."

"The Amoeba has confidence in us," Tod said. "So far we haven't measured up. But we'll get there."

"I'll sleep with Wizard tonight," Vanja said.

"He's not interested in sex," Tod reminded her.

"Not interested *yet*. But he does need reassurance and comfort. I can do these things when I try."

"And here I thought you were a sex machine," Tod said, smiling.

"I *am* a sex machine. But not *only* a sex machine."

Tod nodded. "Thank you, Vanja. If you can help him recover faster, that will benefit us all."

The vampire was as good as her word. She joined Wizard under Bem's blanket, holding his hand and whispering in his ear.

"She'll seduce him if she can," Veee said knowingly. "And if she succeeds, he may indeed recover faster."

"I hope so." Tod put his arms about her. "I could use some comfort too. Maybe before or after the sex."

"Maybe instead of the sex," she said. "I don't have to match her tonight."

"Instead of," he agreed, disappointed.

But she compromised. She comforted him *during* the sex.

In the morning Wizard was significantly improved, though still weak. He was able to get up and walk, and to feed himself. Another day should get him back to par.

They did not ask Vanja whether she had succeeded in seducing Wizard, and she did not volunteer an answer. But later Tod queried Bem privately, as it had been there throughout.

"She did succeed," Bem replied. "But he made her promise not to tell, perhaps because his performance was far less robust than yours. She did most of it herself, until she coaxed it from him."

And they had forgotten that there was another witness to the action. At least Wizard had, and Vanja had not reminded him. That was perhaps her way of letting the others know that she had conquered. That was what counted, with her.

"It may be that she felt her promise included you," Tod said. "So you should treat this matter as private, and not mention it elsewhere. I will do the same."

"An interesting nuance," Bem said. "I shall conform."

But Veee knew anyway, when Tod saw her later. "He wanted to be seduced, without admitting it," she said. "Keeping it private so that if he turned out to be unable to complete it, there would be no embarrassment."

Tod realized that made sense. He would have felt much the same. Wizard was old, but still a man, and Vanja's intimate attention would have reminded him forcefully.

No attack came, that night or the following morning. What was the pool up to?

"I have an idea," Vanja said.

"What, here in public?" Tod asked as if shocked.

She smiled. "Not that. But if you tease me too far, I'll seduce you in public. Again. You know I like an audience when I can get it." She took an impressive breath. "We have displayed our arts, but Wizard has not yet done so."

"I have no art," Wizard protested. "Merely a desire for an art. That is not the same."

"That will do. My idea is while we are waiting for the attack, and the villagers are nervous, to put on an entertainment. A little play, perhaps. You can tell a story, Wiz, and we'll act it out as well as we can, and the villagers can watch and maybe be diverted. The children could use it; they're scared."

"But I can't do that."

"Now be reasonable, dear." Tod saw Wizard start when she applied the term; it was a strong hint that they had been intimate. She was still working him over, in her fashion; Tod appreciated the art of it. "You are physically drained, but not mentally. You can tell a good story."

"I don't have a story!"

Vanja waggled a finger at him. "What, getting stage fright? You have stories, and now is the time."

Wizard sighed, knowing how aptly he was being managed. "I have ideas, yes, but they are not complete. My experience is in magic, not tale telling. I have no proper resolutions."

"Then tell what you have, and we'll ponder resolutions," Vanja said. "This could be an interesting exercise. Maybe the villagers will have suggestions, too. It will become a community effort."

"It's a love story about a man, a woman, and a fog. They—"

"Frog?" Tod asked. "Kissing a frog?"

"Fog. Dense mist. It—"

"Hold that thought," Vanja said. "We must set it up for the villagers. Tod, you're the leader; organize it."

Tod had no choice but to comply. "Veee, get the details of the stage setting from him. Bem, help her set it up. Vanja, help me explain it to the villagers."

"Of course," she agreed.

They walked to the fortress, where the villagers were working. In the center several women were supervising the children, who did indeed look nervous. They had not experienced anything like this before.

Tod clapped his hands. "Your attention, please. We seem to have a while to wait before the siege. We will make a diversion, so you can relax at least briefly. We will animate a story, and will want your opinion on it. No one needs to attend, and we don't want to interrupt the wall building or other preparations, but the children may find it amusing."

"We need that," a village woman muttered. "We are out of regular stories."

"Organize for attendance. We are preparing the stage now. Make sure some remain alert for androids so they can't sneak up on us."

Several women smiled grimly. It was the stress of that alertness that was wearing them down.

Soon Veee's stage was ready. It was a level section by the river, with the audience surrounding it. Wizard sat in a chair in the center. He seemed hesitant to begin.

"Start talking," Vanja stage-whispered. "Or I'll kiss you." She pursed her lips threateningly.

A child laughed. They were already into it.

Thus prompted, Wizard spoke. "I am the Narrator. I will tell the story without participating in it. Pretend I am invisible, and that only you, the audience, can hear me." The children nodded; they understood about narrators, who were there but not there.

"This is a wilderness. There is a mighty wall on one side." Wizard indicated Bem, who formed into a small wall shape. There was a titter. "And an implacable dangerous swamp on the other side." He indicated a marshy puddle. "Two people find themselves stranded here." He indicated Tod and Vanja, who now stood beside him. "They do not know why they are here, or even who they are, because this region is shrouded by the Fog of Forgetfulness. They are aware only of each other and their immediate surroundings. They do know that their only salvation is to escape the fog. But how? The deadly predators of the swamp will consume them if they venture into it, and the wall is too high to scale. They are stuck here."

Tod and Vanja looked at each other. He wore his ordinary clothing, while she had assumed a seeming red dress with a low décolletage and high skirt. Tod spread his hands, and Vanja shrugged. They did not know what to do, either as actors or as characters in the play. He hoped it turned out to be a good story.

"They try to get to know each other," the Wizard continued. "But this is frustrating, because neither can remember anything. So the man brings out his woodwind pipe and plays a melody. The woman hears this, and dances to the music."

Ah. This they could do. Tod played his ocarina, rendering one of his favorite tunes, Edvard Grieg's lovely *Song of the Morning*. Vanja danced. It became a quite pleasant interlude, because it was apparent that the villagers had never heard this music before and were enraptured by it, and Vanja's dance was phenomenal. Thus all ears were on Tod, and all eyes were on Vanja, and both of them were reveling in the cynosure. Tod realized that this was what he and the other members of the team lived for: genuine appreciation of their arts. They were not professionals, but here in the hinterlands their limited skills were sincerely admired.

They finished the interlude, and the narration resumed. "They decide to work to escape the fog and recover their lives. They discover an old waterlogged bench at the edge of the swamp, evidently left by some prior resident." Wizard indicated Veee, who was now lying beside the puddle, her arms and legs extended stiffly at right angles to her torso. She was the bench. There was another titter. "Perhaps if they carry this bench to the wall, they can use it to stand on, and thus be high enough to surmount the barrier, and escape."

Tod and Vanja considered the bench. First they had to extract it from the swamp. He took hold of the shoulder end of it, and she bent down to lift the hip end. In the process she showed a considerable view of her descending breasts. Tod paused, obviously looking, while Vanja pretended to be unaware. There were more naughty titters, augmented by a few adult chuckles. No one in the vicinity could offer a better vista of this nature than Vanja.

They got the bench out of the muck. Now they had to transport it to the wall. Tod heaved it up to his shoulders, awkwardly, because it did not cooperate at all; the limbs remained projecting inconveniently. The legs were on one side, the arms on the other, one of them crossing his face so that he could hardly see ahead. There were more titters.

He stumbled along toward the wall. "But there was a raging river between the swamp and the wall," the Narrator continued. It was actually little more than a shallow trench with a dribble of water in it. "It could be crossed only by stepping on particular firm stones. To misstep would be to fall, and be borne helplessly out to sea where the ocean predators would make short work of him."

Tod stopped, holding the intractable bench. What next?

"The woman sees the problem, and tells him exactly where the first stone is." Vanja squatted beside the river and gestured, pointing to a stone, illustrating what she was saying. Tod stepped forward and put his foot exactly where she said. Then on to the next stone, and the third, successfully crossing despite being largely blinded by the bench. He had not been swept away by the raging torrent.

"Because they are able to work together, they succeed in bringing the bench to the wall." Tod set it down on its hands and knees. "Then he stands on the bench, but still can't quite reach the top of the wall." Tod was glad Veee was strongly built so he could stand on her back. Bem extended a tentacle to indicate how high the top of the wall was. "But then he boosts her up." Tod put a hand on Vanja's plush bottom, raising her a token amount. He paused to look at the audience, reacting to that contact, and there was more laughter. Children everywhere loved naughtiness even if they didn't understand the full ramifications.

"This is finally effective. She scrambles over the top of the wall, then braces herself and reaches down to help haul him up. In this manner they are able at last to pass the obstacle."

The two of them stood beyond the wall, holding hands, exhilarated by their success.

"Now they are beyond the fog. Their memories are returning. They look at each other, appalled. Because now they know that in real life they are of different tribes, implacable opponents who have sought only to kill each other."

Tod and Vanja gazed at each other, trying to signal being appalled. They dropped hands and moved apart. This was as much a surprise to them as actors as to the characters of the story. They had been getting interested in each other. Was it to be abruptly ended?

"Why, then, did they agree to enter the fog? Now they remembered that too: there was a larger threat, to both of their warring tribes. They needed to coordinate to oppose the common menace, if they could, lest both tribes be extirpated. So they had entered the fog together to see if they could get along when there was no history between them. To see if they could interact compatibly to achieve a common goal. They had done so. Now can they do it when their memories are intact?"

Wizard paused for effect, while Tod and Vanja quietly came back together. "But it seems that history is too much. Now that they remember it, all the old grudges come back. 'No way!' he says. 'Never!' she agrees.

Damn. That was not the conclusion Tod wanted.

Vanja stepped into him, put her arms about him, and kissed him ardently. He kissed her back. Thus clasped, they waited.

"Will they work it out?" Wizard asked rhetorically. "Or must they separate, losing their newfound love? That is the question before you. This story is unfinished until you decide."

"How can they?" a man demanded. "They're enemies."

"But they're in love," a woman replied.

The audience dissolved into debate. But the purpose of the story had been accomplished: to give relief from the tension of the coming siege.

They left the scene while the villagers continued their discussion. "You passed," Vanja told Wizard. "You're a tale teller."

"But it has no resolution."

"That is the resolution, for the villagers. That may be your signature. The story that ends in a question."

"Perhaps so," he agreed. "Thank you, vampire."

"Just get physically better. We still have a job to do."

They did indeed. But Tod was glad that the last art had been displayed. The team was complete.

Then came the first report of a missing villager. The man had gone out in the night to urinate, and not returned. His family was alarmed; this was not like him. They made a search, but there was no sign of him, or of foul play. He was simply gone.

Work continued on the fortress. Villagers ranged through the forest, fetching in supplies for a siege. And two more men disappeared. Vanja transformed and did an aerial search, but again, no sign.

"The androids have to be getting them," Tod said. "But how? They know better than to take on any androids alone. And these two were together anyway."

Now the mystery was ugly. This was a new phase of the war, one they did not understand. Somehow the androids were finding a way to take out armed, alert men.

"Damn, I wish we had succeeded in taking the pool out first," Tod muttered. "Now it knows we are out to get it, and it is playing it cagy, maybe invoking some prepared program to take out exactly such a team as ours."

"We tried," Veee reminded him.

"But we tried stupidly, thanks to my inexperience. That just got us in trouble. It was my fault."

"We agreed with you."

"You trusted my judgment. That trust was misplaced."

"I don't think so. It just is turning out to be more complicated than we thought."

"That makes two mysteries," Vanja said. "The crabs that didn't attack, and the missing men. Could they be connected?"

"They were observing," Veee said. "The pool concluded that we like to interact with each other. But how could that translate into missing villagers?"

"Assuming it does translate," Tod said. "They are two parallel things, not directly connected. But it does bear thinking about."

The day clouded over, and light rain came. Tod dug out his folded polyester film raincoat, or more properly a poncho, and put it over his clothing, cinching the hood at his neck. The others lacked such protection but didn't seem to care. Vanja's painted apparel was waterproof, and Veee simply packed away her robe and went nude, as must have been legitimate in her culture. That attracted a number of looks from village men, but she ignored them and they got the message: she was not soliciting their interest. After all, the village women were doing the same; Tod looked and ignored them similarly. Wizard remained under cover, and Bem was impervious.

The two women went out together, honoring their policy of never entering the forest alone, and Tod went with Bem.

They ranged through the forest, eating berries and collecting fallen branches for the defensive fires, helping the villagers. Tod and Bem became separated from the women but remained within shouting distance. Every so often they encountered pairs of villagers, usually men, because the women were encouraged to remain in the safer fortress.

Then they saw something odd. It was a lone dog-sized six-legged android crab, standing motionless. That in itself was not unusual, as the things did not necessarily attack, especially when over-matched; they were more likely to watch and wait while the pool sent reinforcements to surround and overwhelm the prey. But this one was green. All other androids had been orange. What did this color change portend? There had to be a reason, and they needed to understand that reason.

"Go fetch the girls," Tod murmured. "I'll watch this, just as it's watching me."

Bem glided rapidly away, leaving Tod to make sure the oddity did not depart.

Then another person appeared. It was a naked woman, apparently one of the villagers. She was a beauty, with proportions much like Vanja's, and dark hair descending to her waist. He did not remember seeing her before; surely he would have noticed. But she seemed to be in trouble. She stumbled, having difficulty balancing, and was about to fall when Tod jumped to catch her.

She turned to face him, putting her arms about him. She drew him in close, her breasts flatting against his poncho. Then her legs came up to clasp his hips. His arms went around her almost involuntarily. She brought her face to his. She seemed to be after sex, but he was fully clothed. She had not noticed? And why would she want it with a stranger anyway? This was not the way of any remotely normal woman. Vanja, of course, was not normal.

He froze momentarily. Her skin was pasty white, rather than flesh colored. Her features were almost perfect, but her face had no expression. Her eyes were blank. In fact they weren't eyes at all, but bands of white within the eyelids. Her mouth was no mouth, but red lips parted to show a band of white in lieu of teeth. Her nostrils were not open, but sealed off. She was not breathing, and there was no visible pulse in her neck. Even her hair, he saw now, was not hair, but a dark brown mat. She was no human being.

In fact she was an android. A mockup of a woman, convincing from a distance, but an empty manikin up close. He had been completely fooled. He should not have allowed her to touch him.

Then she squeezed. Her arms and legs constricted around him like tightening cables, crushing his chest and belly. He tried to push her away, but she would not be dislodged. He tried to strike her face, but it was leather tough, effectively invulnerable.

He remained on his feet, while she had become a clinging octopus, all limbs tightening around him with inhuman power. He staggered, turning around as he tried to maintain his balance, knowing that if he fell to the ground he would be lost. He might be lost already. But if he could draw his knife and saw at a limb he might save himself.

She relaxed, and he got a breath. But then she constricted again. What was going on? The androids had never been ones to toy with their prey; once they attacked, it was kill or be destroyed.

He spun around again, trying to dislodge her. Again she relaxed, and again tightened. Soon she would cut off his breathing entirely from the constriction of his chest.

Then he realized that she relaxed only when he was facing a particular way: toward the village. He couldn't explain it, but he wasted no time taking advantage of it. He turned again and this time stopped while facing that way.

She hung on him, her limbs loosening, her head falling to the side. He got a hand around and caught one of her arms, pulling it away. Then a leg, and he saw that where it joined her body there was no genital region, merely another white band. She dropped to the ground.

And scrambled back to her feet. She came at him again, trying for the bear hug. Her face remained expressionless. He pushed her away, but she kept coming.

Then he got smart. He jumped to position himself so that she stood between him and the village. She collapsed. This time he followed her down, keeping her body toward the village. She remained inert. He had found a way to disable her, though he had no idea how it worked.

"Tod!" It was Veee's voice.

"Down here!" he called. "I've got an android!"

Then they stood around him: Veee, Vanja, and Bem. "That's some creature," Vanja said.

"It's an android. It's inactive as long as I keep it between me and the village."

"No," Veee said. "As long as you stay between it and the pool."

That made sense. "But why?"

"Now I understand," Bem said. "Androids are in constant touch with their pool. There is a signal animating them. You are blocking that signal."

"That never worked before," Tod said, starting to get up. The android stirred, and he quickly dropped back down.

"You are wearing the poncho," Bem said. "That is a special material."

Tod worked off the poncho. Then he got to his feet, but held the poncho low. The android did not stir. He lifted the poncho, and she came to life. He flung the poncho on her, and she dropped. He moved to the side, no longer between her and the pool, but she did not animate.

"The polyester is finely wrought," Tod said. "Variations are used in photography and insulation. It must block the signal."

"Now we can disable an android without having to hack it apart," Vanja said. "But with only one poncho, that's limited."

"We can cut it up and make patches for each of us," Tod said. "That will help when we're fighting androids. It will make them pause, so we can chop off limbs with less danger."

"A worthwhile discovery," Bem said. "However, we have lost the green crab."

Tod looked. The green android was gone. "I think it was there as a distraction, to give the humanoid time to approach. That certainly worked."

"Now we have seen more of what the pool can do," Vanja said. "It can change colors or forms."

"And now we know what happened to the missing village men," Veee said. "This thing took them out. There may be more than one of it."

Tod shuddered. "But for the poncho, I would have been dead."

"We are seeing the pool's larger potential," Bem said. "If it can emulate a human being well enough to get close enough, what else can it do?"

What else indeed! "We need to have another council of war," Tod said, shaken.

"Meanwhile, what do we do with the body?" Vanja asked.

"I think we have to take it to the village, to show them what they are up against," Tod said. "So that no more villagers are taken out by this device."

"Then what?"

"What are you getting at?"

"We can't just turn the android loose to resume combat," Vanja said. "We have to kill it. Boiling water should do that. But even so we can't just leave it; crabs will grab it and take it back to the pool for recycling. We can't allow that either."

"What are you suggesting?"

"I think we'll have to eat it."

"Eat it!" Tod exclaimed, revolted.

"Think it through, lover. When the fortress is under siege, and nobody can get out, food will get low. Game is already scarce; the androids have cleaned it out. The villagers and we of the team will have to eat something. The one thing we can be sure there'll be plenty of is android flesh. It's made from our flesh, that is, animal flesh; it should be digestible if cooked enough."

She was making ugly sense. "We'll tell the villagers," Tod agreed heavily. "But I hope Wizard recovers quickly, so we can try again to take out the pool. That's the only way we are likely to end this war."

"I hope the big attack on the fortress is done by crabs," Veee said. "I can eat crabs."

Tod had to agree. It might all be android flesh, whatever its form, but the thought of carving and eating humanoid shaped flesh made him nauseous.

CHAPTER 7: POOL

The villagers did not like it any better than Tod did. But they saw the humanoid android come to life when Tod lifted the poncho, and recognized the danger she represented to unwary men. They knew her flesh could not be allowed to return to the pool. So finally they cooked her with hot water and stored her away out of sight. When the siege came, and they got hungry enough, they would reconsider.

Vanja elected to spend another night with Wizard, under the Bem blanket. That left Veee to sleep with Tod. "This makes twice in a row for you," Tod remarked.

"She does not have to keep up with me. I had to keep up with her, until the shares were fixed. They are fixed now, so it does not matter which of us has you."

"I know you're the one for me, Veee, and I want to stay with you. But Vanja—"

She hushed him with a finger to his lips, a gesture that seemed to have lasted 50,000 years. "She enchanted you. You have a passion for her. We know that. When she moves on she will leave you to me, instead of taking you with her. I appreciate that."

"You two are becoming friends."

"Yes, I don't want her to move on. She has courted and won me as a friend."

"And me as a lover."

"She wants you for a friend also, Tod."

"She's a vampire!"

"She's a person. Give her a fair chance."

He shook his head. "You love me, yet you want me to better appreciate my mistress."

Veee smiled. "We live in interesting times." She had learned that comment from him.

"Interesting times," he agreed. Then he kissed her and they made love.

In the morning Wizard was much improved again, and seemed almost back to his original vigor. This time he acknowledged Vanja's help. "She has given me the illusion of, if not youth, middle age," he said.

Bem agreed. "Not as robust as you, Tod, but well beyond the prior night. The vampire needed to do only half of it. His overall health is better, too."

"Give me more nights, and I will make him young," Vanja said, satisfied.

"One more day will return me to full strength," Wizard said. "Then you may return your ministrations to your real lover."

One more day. Then they could bomb the pool. Assuming that Tod could figure out a way to get them there without requiring Wizard's intercession. Wizard would need all his strength for the pool.

The fortress was almost complete, with only finishing touches being made. The villagers had deserted the village and moved to their relatively austere quarters in the fortress. They were ready for the siege.

Again, Tod was not satisfied. "Now we know they can assume human form. Even if not, they seem likely to attack with seemingly overwhelming force. We need a back-up defense in case they breach the wall and get inside the fortress."

"A fire pit," Bem said. "To trap, stun, melt, and dispose of the bodies. That is how we finally prevailed."

"But they'll soon catch on and avoid it," Vanja said.

"Not necessarily. Individually they are stupid; the pool guides them. But in a mass attack, the pool will have dozens of androids to direct. It will be fully occupied, and they will be on their dull own much of the time. We should be able to take out many androids before it catches on."

"We'll do it," Tod agreed.

They got to work, supervising villagers who dug a deep pit, lined it with stones, then piled in brush. "When the attack comes," Tod said, "we'll set fire to the brush and let it burn. By the time it burns out, the rocks will be hot, and they will remain that way for hours. Then if any androids of any type breach our wall, we'll lead them into the pit to burn." He glanced at the women. "Children will be good for that. Train some to scream in front of the androids, then flee around the edge of the pit, leading them in."

Veee and Vanja nodded, and went to talk with women and children. The trap was being set.

Vanja transformed frequently and flew out across the forest, watching. "There is activity," she reported. "I can't see what kind without flying low enough to put myself at risk."

"Don't do that!" Tod exclaimed. "I mean, tactically we can't risk our observer."

"Of course," she agreed, her dark halter fading out momentarily to bare her breasts.

"That too," he agreed, smiling.

The androids did not keep them waiting. Suddenly a force erupted from the forest and charged the circular wall. A small army of six large naked male humanoids, whose arms terminated in sword-like points.

"Fire the pit!" Tod cried. Village women brought torches to do that. "Heat the pots!" And more did that. Suddenly fires were everywhere. "Stand ready at the wall!" The village men were already hurrying to do that, having been alerted by the lookout.

The brute males charged up to the wall and stuck their sword-limbs into it. Their feet were spiked too, so they could climb it. It slowed them, but was no lasting impediment.

But when they did that, they were unable to attack any people. Village men, prepared for this, leaned over the wall and swung heavy axes, cutting off limbs, leaving the androids helpless. Some villagers got right down among them, stabbing and cutting. The androids had to pull out their swords to fight back, but then they couldn't climb. Neither could they readily let go; they had no hands. Before long they had been reduced to armless and legless blobs. More might come, so the defenders couldn't rest, but they were not getting over the wall. It was a standoff.

The fortress had it seemed won the first skirmish. The pool took a while to come up with the next move, and in that time the water pots and fire-pit continued to heat. That was part of Tod's strategy: to hold the androids off long enough with the outer defense so that the inner defense could be established.

Then six more androids came. These were females, like the one Tod had encountered, with splendid bodies and blank faces. They climbed up the backs of the stuck ones and reached the height of the top of the wall. But again they could not strike while they were climbing, and became vulnerable to de-limbing.

But this time the androids were too quick for the defenders, perhaps because it was difficult for men to make themselves dismember voluptuous female bodies. Three reached the top of the wall and started to scramble over.

"Pour!" Tod called.

Now the steaming pots came into play. The villagers tipped them and the scalding water poured out. It bathed the highest androids, cooking those sections it touched, and they collapsed. More androids climbed over them, but got mired in the sogginess below. The villagers chopped at their limbs as the humanoids tried to extricate themselves, but two got through. They strode into the fortress inside the wall.

Now the children sprang to action. They ran in front of the androids, screaming. One android followed; this was what they were programmed to do. She took huge steps, gaining on the children.

Until they reached the central fire pit. One fell in, but the other managed to skirt it. She paused, looking around. She spied Tod watching. She stepped toward him, opening her arms, displaying her breasts.

Until Veee and Vanja charged her from the side, holding up wooden frameworks that rammed into the android, pushing her into the pit. She dropped, and soon smoke rose and the odor of burning flesh spread.

"She thought I would embrace her!" Tod said, amazed.

"Like the prior one," Vanja agreed.

"But we took her out!"

Veee made a gesture of comprehension. "You used your poncho. That interrupted the pool's contact. It couldn't see what happened to her, so it didn't know that ploy was a failure. It's not smart, so it didn't figure out that we had found a way to stop her; she simply vanished from its awareness."

"She went off its radar," Tod agreed. "So it continued to use that ploy."

"Something else," Vanja said. "Those six females were immobile until the males were stopped. Only then did they come to life. Why did the pool space them out like that, when it would have done better if all twelve attacked together?"

Tod suffered a flash of insight. "Bipedal!"

Both women looked at him, not understanding.

"Human beings habitually go on two legs, almost alone in Earth's animal kingdom," he said, excited. "Because it requires a tricky balancing act. We had to develop a brain capable of doing that. Other animals stay on four or more feet to avoid that necessity. So when the pool emulated the human form, it had to make the androids balance, and that's hard. Remember, they have no brains or nervous system of their own. They're just walking meat. So it must be that six is the maximum number the pool can manage before they fall over."

"That does make sense," Vanja agreed. "With six-legged crabs, balance is no problem, but two legs is different."

"It may not have realized just how different until it tried balancing multiple humanoids," Veee said. "But by then it was committed."

"But you bet it will give up on humanoids," Vanja said. "Now that they've failed. The next attack will be crabs, or worse, with no balancing problems."

"Yes, we must prepare for that," Tod agreed.

More androids charged the wall, but now these were indeed

orange crabs evidently held in reserve. They poked their extremities into the fallen ones, hauled them up, and carried them away. "Damn!" Tod swore. "They'll be recycled, and we'll have gained nothing."

"But at least we have held them off," Vanja said, satisfied.

"This time," Bem said. "But the next ones may be twice the size of any prior crabs."

That was a sobering thought. Merely holding off the androids was not going to be enough. They would keep coming back stronger than before, until at last they prevailed.

"We have to take out that pool tomorrow," Tod said.

"I will consult with Wizard tonight," Vanja said. "To see how we can best utilize his magic."

"And I will consult with Bem and Veee to see what non-magical devices we can come up with."

The androids cleared out by nightfall. Apparently their vision was too vague to operate well at night, and they had serious hauling to do. Probably there would be no further attack until daylight.

Nevertheless, the villagers posted lookouts, just in case.

Veee joined Tod for slumber. "This is my last night with you without Vanja," she said.

"You must dread her return."

"No, actually I miss her. Sex is more interesting when she's here."

"You find ordinary sex dull?"

"Yes. What is it, but a particular act? But Vanja somehow makes it novel."

"Will I get in trouble if I agree?"

She laughed. "No, because it's true. Now do you want sex before or after we plan for tomorrow?"

"How about during?"

"As you wish." She got on top of him and took him into her, then was still. "Last time we tried to approach the pool we would have gotten wiped out, but for Wizard. We can't afford to use him that way tomorrow. In fact I think I will carry him, so that he uses up no bodily strength at all. He must be fully charged for the pool."

"You're right," Tod said, intrigued by this mode of discussion. It was pleasant being in her without having to complete it immediately. "But that's a considerable burden to place on you."

"I can do it. I am not sure why the Amoeba selected me for this mission, but maybe it was for this rather than any quality of mind."

"I like your mind," he said, kissing her.

"Thank you." She squeezed his member internally, not enough to set him off. "I have an idea for passing the androids without challenge."

"I thought Wizard could veil us with illusion." He paused. "But that means drawing on his power. I hadn't thought of that."

"Yes. We need to do it without using him at all, until the end."

"Well, there is my poncho, but I'm not sure how that could conceal all of us. It might disable one android, but the others would see us."

"What about masquerading as androids ourselves?"

"Trying to pass as humanoid androids? Wouldn't the pool know it hadn't made us?"

"Does it keep count?"

"I suspect not. But up close we wouldn't look or smell like androids."

"We could make our hair mat, and wear blank expressions. But mainly I think we might smear android juice over our bodies, to make us smell like them. If the pool is concentrating on besieging the fort, it won't be watching us anyway."

"We could pretend to be androids carrying back dead meat for the pool!" Tod exclaimed. "You'll be carrying Wizard. I'll carry Vanja. Or maybe the other way around, if you prefer. Or Bem can carry one. Or Bem can assume a rough crab form and carry a load of dead android. Whatever works. Why would the pool pay any attention to us? Especially if we are among many others doing the same thing."

"Brilliant!" she said, kissing him.

"But you've been doing most of the thinking here."

"No, I am merely encouraging you to be the leader you are. The credit is yours."

"You're trying to make me look better than I am."

"Well, I love you."

Tod thought about that. "A man could get to like a woman who does that for him."

"I like doing it for you."

Something rose in him and spread through his body. "Veee, I want to marry you."

"But what about Vanja?"

"She's fine as my mistress, but I don't love her. I want to have sex with her, but I want to marry you. I love you."

"Thank you," she said faintly.

"Veee, will you marry me?"

"Tod, I can't go with you to your home world."

"Forget my home world! I like this one. Marry me!"

"I would like to. But I think we do not yet know each other well enough to make such a commitment."

"Veee, just say yes!"

"We do not know what the future holds. We may die tomorrow."

"Then let's marry tonight."

"Please, Tod, do not hurry me in this. I love you and want to be with you always, and I do want to marry you, and know you want the same. But we need to be sure it's right. We must give it time."

He knew she was right. "Time," he agreed. "But can we consider it our engagement?"

"Yes, if you wish."

"I don't have a ring to give you, but I'll search for one."

"We can celebrate it this way." Her belly convulsed, and squeezed his member marvelously as she avidly kissed him. He detonated in her, and felt her similar response.

It did seem to be a fitting celebration of the understanding.

Vanja knew the moment she saw them in the morning. "Betrothal! Congratulations. Will there still be a place for me?"

"Mistress," Tod said.

"That will do. You know I will not be bound to any single man." She smiled. "Wizard is now back at full strength. He won't let me tend him any more, but I know he appreciated his time with me."

They told her of their plan to infiltrate the android throng. "Genius!" Vanja said.

"I told you Tod was smart," Veee said.

Vanja glanced shrewdly at her. "And the smartest thing he ever did was to fall in love with you, you delightful primitive."

"Yes!" Tod agreed, and Veee blushed modestly.

They set about masking themselves. Wizard and Vanja would not need it, because they would play the roles of carrion, but the other three did. They hauled up a scorched arm of the feminoid in the pit, melted it in a pot, and spread the goo over their bare bodies. Bem not only spread, it assumed the rough form and color of a giant crab, with six stubby projecting upper limbs. There were not six legs, but the color made it seem as though there were legs there.

The androids attacked. Sure enough, this time the big orange crabs were back. But their limbs were not as good for scaling the wall as the swords and hands of the humanoids had been, and the first wave was repulsed with boiling water and frenzied chopping.

Tod consulted with the village head man. "Can you handle this without us? We need to try again to bomb the pool."

The past few days had given the villagers a lot of savage experience. "We can hold out for a few hours. Then we'll tire and they'll overrun us."

"A few hours is all we'll need. Once we bomb the pool, all the androids should drop dead, in their fashion. If we fail, we'll try to get back here to help you survive."

The man nodded and went back to work, shoring up the weak spots as they manifested. So far, boiling water and swords were doing it. But they all knew that any reprieve would be temporary, because the pool simply recycled the dead androids to make new ones.

Now was the time. Vanja transformed and flew over the fortress, surveying the situation. "There's a kind of gap in the middle," she reported. "Where the attacking crabs are making way for the carrion carriers."

"That's us," Tod agreed. "You know your roles. Get moving, and I'll protect you as I can."

They lined up in the center: an orange crab bearing a live human being, a nude feminoid bearing a live woman, and Tod, a naked male ready for combat or salvage. If anything went wrong, the two unconcealed ones could escape, either by transforming and flying, or by floating up. The three others would form a close group and try to fight their way out. It was a crude strategy, but they were not dealing with genius. It should do.

Then Tod climbed over and dropped to the ground beyond, doing his best to emulate a humanoid android. He knew he had the smell and the appearance; the pool should be able to see him only via the vague vision of the others. If it did not realize that he was not actually being operated by it, this ploy was good.

He stood for a moment, looking around, as if checking for something to attack or carry. The busy orange crabs ignored him. That was promising.

He turned and saw Bern haul Wizard down on its back. Wizard was deliberately inert, exerting no effort of his own, saving all of his strength for the finale. It looked approximately like a giant orange crab with man-shaped carrion on its back. Again, the androids ignored them.

Then Veee slid down, carrying Vanja across her broad shoulders. The vampire wasn't heavy, being a very slender creature, sylph-like compared to the muscular Veee, and of course she was unobtrusively holding on so that Veee's hands were free to steady herself. Tod admired them both in their separate fashions: the one with muscular arms and legs along with broad hips and large breasts, the other hardly two thirds her weight with her smaller hips and breasts that seemed more pronounced because of the slenderness of the rest of her body. Had he been selecting women from a picture catalog, he would have chosen Vanja immediately. But he had come to know them both, and while he had a continuing passion for Vanja, he loved Veee. The men of her world might have found her unattractive, but Tod had come to know her better, and she was the one for him. Having both women together was as close to paradise as he was likely to get. He was immensely pleased that the two had become friends, and that neither was the jealous type. In fact he loved the way the two collaborated to arouse and satisfy his passion as often as they could.

This reflection took only an instant while he waited to be sure the androids had not been alerted. The things were not subtle enough to pretend acceptance in order to get the whole party among them so that the prey was vulnerable, but the pool just might be, so it remained nervous business. The route seemed clear.

Tod spied a de-limbed crab that was small enough to carry. It was inert; the pool did not bother animating flesh that had become useless. Tod picked it up and slung it over one shoulder. This completed his disguise. One thing about android flesh: it didn't bleed. It was like a fleshy toy.

They moved out, forging with deliberate clumsiness past the androids and into the forest. There was a rough line of live androids carrying dead androids; they fit right in. Tod led the way with his burden, followed by Bem, followed in turn by Veee.

The path was now well worn by the many feet of the androids, easy to follow. They tramped on without pause. Tod got nervous when they approached the place where the androids had ambushed them before, but this time they passed it without event. So either they pool had not caught on, or whatever challenge there was would occur later.

They passed a rise and started down. Soon that reversed, and the route became steep. Now they really had to work to bear their burdens up the slope. The androids were indefatigable; the team members had to conceal their weakness as much as possible. They were surely getting close.

They crested a rocky ridge. And there it was: a declivity in the hills, forming a small high valley whose base the pool had filled in. Tod saw what looked like a lake of goo, brownish on one side, orange on the other. The pool!

There was activity there. Androids were carrying their loads to the edge and unceremoniously dumping them in at one side. From the other side shapes were emerging: the new androids. Apparently they formed beneath the surface, and when they were complete, marched out to get to work. They were orange, matching that section of the pool.

Now the line of androids halted. They dumped down their burdens and departed along another path.

Tod was dismayed. Why weren't they delivering directly to the pool? Now he saw that the androids that were delivering were a different group, coming out from the pool to pick up the offerings and bear them on in. It was a simple relay, probably more efficient than having one set of androids proceed all the way from the siege area to the pool. But it represented an unexpected and formidable obstacle. Tod could throw down his offering, but Bem could not dump Wizard. The inner circle androids might routinely chop him up for the occasion and dump the pieces into the pool.

What were they to do? They couldn't dawdle any length of time, as that would soon arouse suspicion. But neither could they complete their journey to the pool.

He formed an instant plan, hoping it would not turn out to be a disaster. "Bem, Vanja. Join with me to make a distraction that takes the androids' or the pool's attention for a few minutes. Veee, dump down your load the way the others do, and remain in place. When the distraction occurs, pick up Wizard as if you are one of the inner circle androids, and carry him down to the pool. Act as if this is your assignment." He took a breath. "In case things go wrong, remember I love you." He paused. "Now!" He threw his own carcass down.

Bem slid Wizard onto the ground beside the other carrion, and slid back, changing form and colors.

Veee nodded. She dumped Vanja down.

Vanja landed on her feet. "Hey, I'm not going there!" she exclaimed, and ran toward Bem. She jumped on Bem's back. "Take me away from all this garbage, my loyal steed!"

If their appearance and actions had not alerted the pool, surely their voices did. Androids might hear, but they did not talk. The nearest ones oriented on Bem and Vanja.

"This way!" Tod cried, waving his arms violently as he ran up toward the ridge.

Bem and Vanja followed. So did the androids. With luck the pool's attention was on them, reorganizing them to give pursuit, not noticing what remained behind. Tod regretted that he could not watch to see what happened, but he could not risk having an android look too.

Tod crested the ridge and ran down the other side. Bem and Vanja were right after him, the vampire making a siren sound that was probably audible throughout the region. She was one ham actress!

The androids charged over the ridge. They could not actually move as rapidly as Tod and Bem could, being constructed for combat and carrying, but they were brisk enough. "Keep them close," Tod called. "But don't let them catch you. The way we did with the wolfkeys when we swam to the island." Only there was no android-eating predator to intercept them.

They ran into the forest and dodged among the trees. But now more androids were coming from the other direction. The pool was summoning all the closest ones, and they were surrounding the fugitives in their classic hunting pattern. This was mischief.

"Climb!" Tod cried, and scrambled up a giant tree trunk. He knew the androids could climb, but not well. The fugitives should be able to fend them off.

Bem slid right up the tree, carrying Vanja along. When they were above Tod, she got off and started climbing on her own. When Tod looked up, she changed her costume so that she appeared to be wearing a short skirt without panties. Her flexing legs showing everything. She just couldn't stop teasing him, even in potentially dire straits like these.

Tod focused on the job at hand, and climbed. Soon the three of them were high above the forest floor, safe for the moment.

"We'd better keep taunting them," Vanja said. "So they don't give up the chase too soon." She peered down through the branches, "Hey, you orange freaks! Bet you can't catch us! How'd you like a taste of this meat?" She flashed her legs at the slowly climbing crabs.

"I think Bem and I can handle it," Tod said. "You should go check on Veee and Wizard."

"You're right." She shifted to full nudity and transformed, flying away.

"Human courtship continues to be interesting," Bem remarked. "Is she aware that you can't conveniently indulge in copulation with her at the moment?"

"She's aware. She's an inherent tease." Tod did not care to admit to either Vanja or Bem how effective that teasing was. Seeing up her mock skirt that way... "Let's cooperate in fending off the androids. If I use my poncho to stun them momentarily, can you cut off key limbs?"

"I can," Bem agreed, forming a giant set of pincers. Tod hadn't seen those before; Bem must have been thinking about how better to deal with the crabs.

The first crab reached their branch. Tod angled his poncho to put it between the android and the pool. It froze in place. Bem, glued to the trunk, extended the pincers down and crunched off the limb with the spike wedged in the branch.

The android dropped to the ground, crashing through the foliage and bouncing off the crabs below.

"That was satisfying," Tod said.

"I agree."

The next crab came up, and they dispatched it similarly. Then a third. "They don't seem to realize their attack's not working," Tod said.

"I believe the pool is concentrating on the siege of the fortress, while these ones are on repetitive instructions."

"Autopilot," Tod agreed. "Let's hope Veee and Wizard are encountering similar inattention."

The bat returned and transformed into the woman, her bare legs spreading above Tod as she clung to the tree. She leaned down to ensure that her breasts were also fully displayed. "Bad news. There's a defensive trench around the pool, allowing access at only one place, and that's a second carrion hand-off station. Veee can't pass it. I could help boost Wizard through, but they would notice and converge. We need another distraction."

"Damn!"

She waggled a finger at him. "You stopped me from using vulgar language, Tod; you shouldn't use it yourself."

"Is this flirting?" Bem inquired.

"You bet," Vanja said, smiling.

"We'll have to help them," Tod said. "Bem, you make a distraction so I can get down off this tree. Is there a crab-free route I can take?"

"Over the ridge, there," Vanja said, pointing. "It's off the path; no androids there. You can get most of the way to the pool before they spot you. But they're quite alert near the pool; no pre-programmed units there. You could get hurt."

Tod was sure that was so. He might not get through. "Bem, can you camouflage yourself so you can reach Veee unobserved, if I draw the androids' attention?"

"I may be able to."

"Then after you distract them so I can get off the tree and over the ridge, you disappear and go to Veee. Help her get Wizard to the pool, or take him yourself." He turned to Vanja. "Guide me, help me, and if they overwhelm me, transform and escape. I am expendable."

"Not to me," she said. She leaned down farther and kissed him. "I'll guard your back as you descend."

"Move!" Tod started down the tree. A crab was there. He shaded it with the poncho and scrambled right by it, so that when it recovered it was above him and seemingly unaware that he was gone. But there was another below. He shaded that one, but could not get by it until Vanja got between them and bit its supportive limb. That rendered it inoperative, allowing Tod to pass.

Meanwhile Bem, above, made its siren whoop and fell out of the tree in the form of a big brightly colored ball. It bounced on the ground, then rolled downhill, flashing and whooping. That got the androids' attention and they swarmed after the ball.

Tod dropped the rest of the way to the ground. There were no crabs there for the moment.

"This way," Vanja said, and ran obliquely up the slope. Tod followed. At least now she was not playing her seductive games.

Then her bottom flashed white, as if uncovered by a flouncing skirt. She had not forgotten.

Beyond the ridge it was all downhill. Now Tod saw the trench around the pool, with the androids crossing it at the single shallow section. Another simple yet effective defense. The pool's ancestors must have had experience and found out what worked, and now it was automatic.

He no longer heard the whooping. That meant Bem was shifting from attention-drawing to disappearing. Bem would get Wizard there as long as Tod distracted the androids. He needed to get close enough to gain the attention of the ones near Veee, yet far enough so that he could escape them. But he feared that combination was not going to be feasible.

He came as close as he dared. "Yahooo!" he called, waving at the orange throng.

They did not respond. What was the matter?

"They don't see us as a threat," Vanja said. "So they're continuing their business."

"Well, I'll take care of that." Tod ran toward the trench. He slid into it. It was about eight feet deep. The slopes were too steep and hard for him to climb, as he had known they would be. "Boost me up."

Vanja took hold of his ankles and heaved him up. She was surprisingly strong, considering her appearance; that must be part of her vampire heritage.

His hands reached the rough inner edge of the wall, but did not find purchase. "Farther," he said.

"Can't." She lowered him.

Then he saw why: a giant crab was coming for them.

"Take the poncho," Tod said, handing it to her. "Put it between the android and the pool."

She obeyed, and the crab went dead. Tod scrambled up onto its back and reached again for the top of the slope, but it still wasn't enough. Then Vanja draped the poncho over the android and joined him on it. She heaved on his ankles again, and this time got him far enough up to catch hold and scramble on out. "Thanks!"

"Catch!" she called, and heaved the balled poncho up to him.

He caught it. "But what about you?"

She transformed and flew up to perch on his shoulder. oh. He had for the moment forgotten.

Now the androids oriented on him in a mass. He had become a seeming threat to the pool. They charged in from either side.

"Yahooo!" he repeated, running down toward the pool, waving his arms. Had he given the others enough time?

More androids swarmed from the direction of the pool. They surrounded him, closing in. "Take off, bat brain!" he exclaimed. "Go help the others, I'm done here."

"No. We can fight them," she said, transforming. "Stand back to back, and wield your poncho."

They tried it, but it wasn't enough, because they weren't facing each other and he couldn't nullify the ones on her side. The orange crabs pressed in closer, and Tod knew the end was only seconds away.

"Get out of here!" he cried. "I've got one last ploy!"

"I love you." That was a verbal flash, and it affected him more strongly than the visual flashes had, because he knew she wasn't teasing. She was a tough-minded predator, but she had come to care for him, as he had for her.

Then the bat was flying up, and a bull-sized crab was upon him. Tod cried out and threw himself on its back. Its arms closed about him and he went completely limp, playing dead. With luck it would treat him as it would a carcass, and not stab him. All it needed to do was carry him to the nearby pool.

That was what it did. The other crabs fell back, no longer needed. They were used to dealing with carrion; its proper function was to be transported to the pool for processing. So he had won that gamble. Now all he needed to do was avoid getting thrown into the pool, to be dissolved and recycled. He saw it coming closer. He also saw the bat hovering close, unable to help him.

His captor stopped behind another crab. They were at the brown portion of the pool, the entry port. The other crab tossed in another crab, one that had been de-limbed. It entered the pool without a splash, merely making a low slow wave as it sank part way, then rose again, floating mostly submerged. Thick bubbles formed around it, popping and releasing noxious gas as the flesh was liquified. The corpse dissolved visibly from the outer edge as it was digested. It seemed that the pool could process only so much at a time, hence Tod's brief reprieve.

A waft of vapor passed them. Tod's host did not react, as it did not breathe, but Tod choked on the stink. Rotten eggs, liquid turds, week-old vomit, putrid cheese—he had to hold his breath until it passed, lest he puke out his guts before the pool got them. What a stench!

The carrion sank under the roiling surface. At last he could breathe again! He looked around with stinging eyes. And there on the other side was another orange crab carrying Wizard. So they had lost that ploy too.

No. That wasn't an android. *It was Bem masquerading as an android*. They had made it after all!

Tod's crab lifted him up and made ready to heave him into the pool. He came to life and spread out his poncho, halting it. But now the others were pressing back in, as the pool caught on to the danger. They reached for him—

There was a weird deep-set thud. Then a geyser erupted from the pool, rising high and spreading, forming a roiling mushroom shaped cloud. The surface of the pool was boiling as thick brown gas escaped. The amplified fetor was overpowering. And all the androids collapsed.

Wizard had bombed the pool. The substance was still there, but now it had lost its animating force. It was merely protoplasm that would soon rot and become plant food.

They had won.

CHAPTER 8: SEARCH

They rested by the edge of the village, which was now being restored. Wizard, depleted again, was supported by a plush easy chair that was Bem's current form. Tod was supported by a row of four breasts, as the two women knelt behind him and held him close. He had taken more of a beating than he had realized during the throes of battle, and did need recovery time. There were large bruises on his limbs and torso, and his right shoulder was painful to move beyond a limited range. He had tried to protest their attentiveness, but they had insisted, and his objections were not strong. He loved the feel of their warm bodies against him; every breath they took reminded him anew.

"Well, I guess we succeeded," Tod said. "It wasn't pretty, and certainly there was no genius plan, but we managed to bungle through and get the job done."

"It succeeded because of your leadership, strategy, and execution," Wizard said. "It was not required to be pretty."

"Still, I made so many errors of judgment along the way, I'm embarrassed. It was a victory, yes, but a largely bungled one, owing a huge amount to simple luck."

"Actually luck is a kind of magic in some frames," Wizard said. "Perhaps you possess it."

"I'm not from a magic frame."

"Hence you never had prior opportunity to discover that quality," Wizard said. "Regardless, the Amoeba selects a team that can do the designated task. It does not require it to be genius or even competent, merely adequate. We, as a team, proved to have the required qualities."

"We were similarly clumsy in our victory in my frame," Bem said, the sound seeming to come from around Wizard. "I suspect the Amoeba does not have a choice from among top performers, but from among those that are somehow dissatisfied with their situations and so are ready to take the trail."

"We were the best of a bad lot," Tod said, and both women laughed. That made his head rock pleasantly.

"An exaggeration," Wizard said. "We may not have been the top picks, but we have formidable capacities. Also, the capacity of the team may be beyond the sum of the capacities of its members. We do seem to work well together."

"Unified by our arts," Veee said.

Tod shrugged. "However, we know the job is not finished. We took out the pool, but we don't know its origin. We need to locate and deal with that, to prevent any recurrence."

"We do," Bem agreed.

"We can be pretty sure the pool did not originate on the trail," Wizard said. "It has to have come from an off-trail realm."

Vanja laughed again. "And that leaves a mere all space, all time, and all alternate universes to consider."

"Child's play," Veee agreed.

"I doubt it," Wizard said. "I believe we should start by checking our home frames."

"But we didn't bring any androids!" the vampire protested. "We'd have noticed."

"Not us specifically, but someone else from our frames. Maybe one of the local villagers, or a member of some other village."

"Why?" Veee asked. She seemed not to be arguing—she seldom argued about anything—but was genuinely curious.

"Because in my observation the Amoeba follows the path of least resistance, like water flowing downward. It is easier to make an offshoot from an existing trail than to fashion an entirely new one. The preponderance of human beings here suggests that an early trail brought one human in, and subsequently offshoots brought in others for other missions. Bem is the only completely nonhuman entity we have seen, though there are surely others farther along the trail. So a branch from one of our trails is our most likely suspect."

Veee nodded. "That makes sense to me."

"And to me, grudgingly," Vanja said. "I note our party of five has three full humans, one half human, and one alien thing. So chances are about three and a half out of five that the guilty trail is pure human."

"Or seventy percent," Tod said.

"Exactly," Wizard said. "That narrows down the suspects."

"However," Bem said, "There was an android episode in my frame a few years back. We quelled it, but part of it might have escaped to the trail. That makes my frame a prime suspect. It should be investigated first."

"That makes sense," Veee agreed.

"But not until Wizard recovers," Vanja said. "We might need him to bail us out or bomb something, if we get into more mischief. He needs two more days."

"And you are going to see that he is well taken care of," Veee said.

"Naturally. It's a dirty job, but it has to be done."

"While I struggle to satisfy Tod's limitless passion alone," Veee said severely.

"Well, I suppose we could switch places for a night, for variety or relief."

"No, I will struggle through," Veee concluded.

Tod exchanged glances with Wizard. Both managed to keep straight faces.

"The variations of courtship seem endless," Bem remarked. "Hitherto I had not appreciated the intricacies of teasing."

Then they all laughed.

They helped the villagers move back to their original site. The villagers were duly grateful, and several maidens hinted by glances and flirts of their skirts that they would be happy to take Tod off Veee's hands for a night, but Tod firmly demurred.

"You could do it," Veee murmured in the evening as she massaged his sore shoulder. She was good at it; she seemed to have the healing touch. "I have no restrictive claim on you, and I am not the jealous type. I'm sure they would try very hard to please you."

"I love you."

"And I love you. But we have an open relationship."

"Because of Vanja," he agreed.

"Because we are in the Amoeba. We can have no relationship outside it, and when this mission is done we must return to our home worlds, and we will not see each other any more."

Tod stiffened. "Is this what you want?"

She did not answer immediately, but he felt a warm drop on his back. It was a tear.

"Come down here," he said.

She lay on him, her breasts at his back, her face pressing close to his face, side by side.

"I don't want to go home," he said. "I want to stay here with you. On any basis you prefer, sharing sex or not, just so we can be together. We don't have to go home; we can stay, as the villagers' ancestors did, and live off the land."

"Yes," she breathed. "But Tod, you like adventure. Will you not get bored?"

"With you, never. With primitive village life, probably so. I'm still pondering that aspect."

"Whatever you want, I want," she murmured.

He kissed her, their lips meeting at an angle. Then he rolled over, and she rolled on top of him, clasping him face to face. They did not have sex this time; they didn't need to. It was definitely love.

But what about boredom? Tod knew better than to assume that love would tide them through a useless existence. He had been through this before discovering the trail. He had thought having a lovely loving woman to come home to would alleviate his dissatisfaction with life, but now he know that this would not have been enough. It wouldn't be enough with Veee, either, or even with Veee and Vanja together, because sex was only part of his interest. When this mission for the Amoeba was done, as it seemed soon would be the case, they would be on their own again, on or off the trail, and it would in time become deadly for all three of them. Because they all craved more than sex, more than art, and, yes, more than friendship. They needed a sufficient challenge, something vital to accomplish. They had tasted real adventure, dealing with the android menace, and needed something to match that. What could it be? As yet he had no answer.

When Wizard was better, they organized for the search, starting with Bem's frame. They trekked to the mountain intersection where they had first encountered Bem, and considered the steep descent.

"There will be no problem," Bem said, forming into a shape like a toboggan. The four others sat on this and gripped the provided handholds. Then they slid slowly down the steep slope. Bem had it under control. When it evened out below, the ride continued, taking them though a landscape with forms like mounded colored plastic. This was evidently Bem's native flora.

Bem glided to a halt. "We must converse," it said.

The others got off and formed a circle around Bem, who resumed its normal blob shape. "We will help in any way we can," Tod said. "But you know we can't enter your realm."

"That may be a matter of interpretation," Wizard said. "The Amoeba is familiar with the problem of access and has developed certain protocols to facilitate it when necessary. It can connect us to Bem's presence so that we can see, hear, and feel it, and communicate with it, though Bem's associates in its realm will not be aware of our participation."

"Telepathy?" Tod asked.

"No. We can't contact Bem's mind. But what Bem speaks we will hear, and Bem will hear us. It is awkward to explain."

"Like a bat snooping on humanoids," Vanja said.

"Or a video/audio camera tracking someone," Tod said.

"Or a ghost presence," Veee said.

"These analogies are all imperfect," Wizard said. "But I believe close enough. So if Bem requires our input, we can provide it."

"I may," Bem said. "I need to clarify an aspect of my culture. The cultures of the rest of you are fundamentally material, with goods and power defining the welfare of individuals. Bem culture, in contrast, is artistic. We are motivated by the design, construction, and function of esthetic monuments, and seek always to preserve them. I am not sure your cultures have equivalent terms."

"Architecture," Tod said. "The building of anything from a crap shack to the Eiffel Tower."

Bem considered, digesting the translation. "Yes. I am a chief architect. I must make of our people a unified artifact-that will withstand the next storm of entropy. It is no easy thing."

"A most interesting concept," Wizard said. "In my frame, entropy is that quality of disorder that allows no independent structures. Maximum randomness and uselessness. A storm might blow apart a house, rendering it into a disordered pile of boards. Entropy is not a storm in itself, but can be the result of a storm."

"That is similar. In my frame, entropy is not passive," Bem said. "It actively attacks the ordered structures of civilization and seeks to reduce them to disorder."

"So the laws of physics or magic differ in your frame," Wizard said. "You have organized disorder, oxymoronic as it may seem."

"Active inactivity," Tod said.

"Artless art," Veee said.

"Just as you have bloodless blood," Vanja said. "We're used to different sets of rules. We'll make do."

"Different in every frame, it seems," Bem agreed. "Just so long as you understand."

"You said you have to make a thing of your people," Veee said. "Do you mean for your people, or by your people?"

"Both. But also of them. Every person in our society is part of the artistic whole. If that whole is lost, all will perish." Bem paused. "I felt I was not up to the task, so rather than let my people down, I departed. Now I must return, at least temporarily."

"Temporarily this time," Wizard said. "Permanently, in a few days."

Bem flashed negative colors. "I do not wish to wipe out my people because of an inadequate design or application. Better to vacate my role and allow it to be filled by my sibling, who is more competent than I am."

Wizard shrugged. "My scries are not always completely accurate. I may be mistaken."

"I am not sure of that," Bem said. "At any rate, when I re-enter my frame, I will seek out my sibling to advise it of the necessity to prepare to assume the role. Then I will try to locate the source of the android menace, if it is in my frame."

"You will be able to sniff it out," Wizard said. "Literally. You now know the smell of the androids. If that odor is not present, you will know it is not your frame. If there is only a slight smell, it will suggest that the menace stems from a closely related frame, that we will then have to identify and deal with."

"How will be do that?" Veee asked.

"We will go back along the trail, checking closely for offshoots we missed before. If the androids stem from this vicinity of space/time/reality, there will be an open trail, however obscure."

"Will I be able to visit a realm that is not my own, however proximate it may be?" Bem asked. "I understand that a person loses substance away from its realm."

"That depends on how close to your home frame it is," Wizard said. "The closer it is, the more substance you will possess. I do not know the exact ratio."

"Suppose it's not close enough?" Tod asked.

"That won't matter. We don't need to enter it, we just need to identify it. Then we can verify which inhabitant of the Amoeba associates with it, and persuade that person to go home and stay there, so that the trail dries up. It's not a complicated business."

"Famous last words," Tod muttered under his breath.

"At any rate, when I revisit my home frame, the landscape may seem strange to you," Bem said, speaking to them all. "Do not be concerned. If there is a problem, I will voice it, and you may advise me as you see fit."

"We'll do that," Vanja said.

They moved on. The lumpy landscape became lumpier. Then abruptly Bem went on while they were balked; the trail had ended. "Good luck," Tod said.

"What is luck?"

"A randomly favorable turn of events, enabling you to succeed."

"That is interesting. It does not exist in my frame."

"It surely does exist," Wizard said. "Your folk merely don't recognize it as such."

"That may be," Bem agreed guardedly. It put on its presentation colors and moved out.

Tod found that he was able to watch it advance into its frame. There was no special equipment, nothing he had to do; it was just that when he looked in Bem's direction, he saw Bem as if it were only a few feet away, as though the end of the trail were a big screen showing a three dimensional picture of Bem.

"Remarkable," Vanja murmured. "So we do have a way to visit other frames, at least in spirit."

"The Amoeba is capable of remarkable things," Wizard said. "We have yet to appreciate them all."

Bem came to what was evidently a settlement. Similar bems stood in a broad and lovely pattern, like flowers on a field, each seining the air for nourishment. Some were red, some blue, some yellow, and the pattern vaguely resembled a larger flower. A living blossom, enhanced by the small motions of the seinings, as if a wind were rippling through. In fact the seinings were coordinated, occurring with the same cadence, like the aligned strokes of the bows of violins in a classy orchestra. That was of course no accident. This was a work of art.

"Bem wasn't fooling," Veee murmured. "They are all parts of a picture."

Bem passed through this pattern carefully, gliding from one ring of flowers to another, assuming the color of whatever flower was appropriate, so as not to interrupt the pattern. Tod knew it was Bem, because the focus was on it; otherwise Bem would have been immediately lost amidst the picture.

"I envy Bem's coloring capacity," Vanja said. "I am limited to clothing."

"Yours is just fine," Tod said.

She flashed a bare breast at him, appreciatively.

Bem proceeded to a neighboring pattern, similar to the first but not identical. In fact there were many designs, grouped into a larger pattern of intricate yet lovely complexity. It seemed that all the bems were part of it, and that this was their naturals state.

It reminded Tod of something he had seen. Then he got it: "The Mandelbrot set!"

"Fractals," Wizard said. "A marvelous example. Mathematical artistry."

"I do not know your reference," Veee said, "but I take your meaning. This goes beyond the beauty of the form."

"I never really appreciated paintings," Vanja said. "Until now. This is awesome."

Indeed it was. Bem had said that its culture was artistic rather than material. This was the proof of that. The bems seemed to desire nothing more than to fulfill the larger pattern.

"I wonder whether this is what Heaven looks like," Tod asked rhetorically.

"It must be," Veee agreed softly.

Bem made its way to the center of the larger pattern of this region. There was a black bem that seemed to be the linchpin of the artistic structure.

"Beobrumemmik!" the other said, recognizing Bem.

"The same, Sibling," Bem agreed.

"Are you returned at last to relieve me of this chore?"

"No, Sibling. Merely to inform you that I do not wish to return. You must carry it forward."

"But I am not competent! When the storm comes, I will prove to be inadequate."

"No, Sibling. You are more adequate than I. That is why I departed: so as not to destroy our people and our culture by my failure to accomplish the necessary art. You have a better chance to accomplish it than I do."

"No, Sibling! Standing here in your stead I have come to appreciate the depth of my own inadequacy. I am unable to fulfill the role, and must vacate."

"But you must fulfill it, for I can not."

"Touch me, Sibling, and compare our qualities. You will have the proof."

Bem extended an extension and touched the other.

Tod felt the connection. It was as if he were clasping hands with another person. But this was more than touching physically; he was picking up on the mental state of the other. Sibling was deeply uncertain.

"You seem competent to me, Sibling."

"I am not! The first minor entropy storm of the series will strike soon; tarry long enough to appreciate me in action, and you will know."

"How soon?"

"In two hours. I can handle this one, but you will see the flaws in my capacity that would defeat me in a more serious storm."

"Team?" Bem asked, and it was evident that the sibling did not hear it. Bem was addressing the members of the Amoeba's team.

Tod exchanged glances with the others. "We can wait two hours," Tod said. "You must ascertain how badly your people need you. You would not care to desert them if you knew it made their destruction likely."

"True," Bem agreed. Then, to the sibling: "I will return here in two hours and navigate the entropy storm in parallel with you. We shall see whether my decisions are any better than yours."

"And if they are?"

Bem made a flashing sigh. "Then I will return also for the larger storms."

"Gratitude!"

"But I doubt they will be, Sibling. You have had the same training as I, and have the same native capacity. You should do as well as I."

"I lack that confidence."

"So did I," Bem said. "That is why I departed."

"But you are superior to me now. I can feel it in your very presence. You have changed, Beobrumemmik."

"I do not see why. I merely visited other regions and made new friends. I undertook no special training and did not ponder the situation."

"Nevertheless, I feel that change. You have matured in ways that are inaccessible to me."

Bem shrugged and glided away, shifting colors as it intersected other parts of the pattern. "Now I am sniffing for android traces," it said. "I am not finding them."

Tod was surprised to receive an odor of warm plastic clay, and saw that the others were too. Not only were they seeing, hearing, and feeling what Bem did, they were smelling what Bem smelled. Indeed, there was no android odor here.

"Get to a breezy place," Wizard suggested. "There will be more smells on the winds, from farther afield."

Bem glided rapidly toward a nearby mountain. Tod was amazed by the velocity it could achieve; it was faster than a man could run. He had tended to think of Bem as slow, like a giant snail, despite knowing better; now he saw how fast the creature could move when it tried.

Not only that. Because Bem was traversing the fringes of the area pattern, the flower bed as it were, it was now shifting colors as fast as it moved. It was as if a tiny ripple of air was crossing the pattern, twitching petals here and there without seriously disturbing them. The larger artistry was not interrupted.

Then Bem got beyond the patterns, into the rougher territory beyond. Here there was no real path, merely a tormented landscape of jumbled boulders. Yet Bem navigated this, too, at speed.

"I think we did not know you well enough, Bem," Veee said. "In your own framework, you are a remarkable creature. Your art is as impressive as your physical and mental capacities."

"Thank you, Veee," Bem replied as it sped along. "I have come to appreciate your own art, and that of the other members of the team. More than that, I have learned to relate to the marvels of your courtship and mating protocols, which are of course unknown among my own kind."

"How does your kind reproduce?" Vanja asked. "Surely individuals die on occasion, and need to be replaced."

"We grow, slowly, until we are of sufficient size," Bem said. It was now coming to the base of the mountain, whose surface was smooth and glassy. There were fewer others here, and that pattern was diffuse. "Then we fission, forming two smaller individuals from our substance. Sibling and I are the progeny of the elder individual before us. Our capacities are thus very similar."

"What, no sex?" Vanja asked teasingly.

"Sometimes two of us will merge to form a larger entity, facilitating fissioning. That is a very intimate association, equivalent to your sexual embrace."

"More than equivalent. Do you lose your personal identities?"

"No. They merge like our bodies, forming a more complete one, which will then be shared by our offspring."

"You and your sibling are architects," Tod said. "Was your progenitor of the same persuasion?"

"Yes. The larger patterns of our society require a number of more specialized abilities to complete their forms, and this is ours." Bem was now sliding rapidly up the slope, leaving the others of its kind below.

"Somewhat the way the Amoeba needs several differing individuals to make up a team," Wizard said.

"I appreciate the parallel," Bem agreed. It reached the breezy rounded top of the mountain and seined the air. "I still discover no trace of android."

Tod's nose confirmed it. He would never forget the rank stink of android flesh. There was only fresh clean plastic here. He saw that the others agreed.

"It seems that your frame is not the origin of the androids," Wizard said.

"I had feared it was, because of the android menace we faced before," Bem said.

"You evidently dealt with that so well that no trace remains," Wizard said. "And your frame was not the origin of it. It must have been another victim of a randomly spreading pool."

"I am relieved," Bem said, starting back down the mountain. "I would not have wanted to inflict such a scourge upon any other realm."

"Navigate your storm," Vanja said, "then return to us. We like you, Bem. I never said that to an alien monster before."

"And I like you, Vanja. I never said that to a humanoid before, let alone a vampire."

"Too bad you're not male. I could give you such a good time."

"I fear that state is beyond my ability to achieve. I could assume the approximate male form, and emulate a courtship protocol, but I would be unable to truly copulate or generate a nascent creature with you."

"Maybe you just need more practice."

"You are flirting with me!" Bem said, surprised.

"Well, you know how it is with bems and femmes. They are oddly attracted to each other."

"Odd, indeed," Bem agreed.

Vanja, of course, would flirt with anything, and seduce it if she could. It was nevertheless a signal of the unity their team had formed. They all liked each other, and were happy to interact in various ways, sex not excluded.

Now the first signs of the storm manifested. The flowers moved uncomfortably as if being shaken by small tremors, and the pattern seemed to be distorting. There seemed to be no strong wind there; it was something else.

Bem arrived back in the center. Sibling had not moved. They

touched again, like another handclasp, and held it. "You take the left half," Bem said. "I will take the right."

The storm intensified. Not wind, not an earthquake, not thunder or rain, yet it seemed to have aspects of all of them. Tod tried to analyze it, to fathom what was occurring. It was more like a psychic disturbance whose physical manifestations were merely the reactions of the bems making the flowers. They stood in place, but they wavered. Tod felt as if he were wavering too, though he stood outside it.

"We're feeling Bem's input," Veee said.

"This may not be telepathy," Vanja said, "but it has a certain affinity."

"It is part of the ambiance the Amoeba provides," Wizard explained. "It seems to be a psychic storm, and Bem experiences certain reactions to it, and Bem's body responds, and we pick up on those responses."

Now a more forceful ripple crossed the pattern. Bems rocked back and forth as it struck them, struggling to hold their places. To lose ones place, Tod understood, was to suffer a psychic injury.

"Steady!" Bem's light message radiated. Sibling's message echoed Bem's; they were acting in tandem. It was more than a message; the strength of their encouragement infused the individuals, unifying them, making them stronger. But as the wave crossed the pattern, some of the placeholders did lose their positions, at least to the extent of bending too far to the side so that the pattern was distorted.

It was the entropy, trying to take apart the pattern, to reduce it to disorder and chaos.

"I am beginning to understand," Veee said. "Their art is a bulwark against dissipation. If that goes, they will not survive."

"We struggle physically," Vanja agreed. "They struggle psychically."

"It may seem intangible to us," Wizard said. "But it is their deadly reality."

Tod saw that all the distortions occurred on Sibling's side. Bem was indeed maintaining the pattern better.

Then the wave passed, and the bems relaxed. The pattern had been damaged but not broken. The errant individually quickly returned to their proper stances.

"You held better than I did," Sibling said. "You are stronger than I."

"How can that be, when we are twins?"

"You have changed, as I said. I have not."

"Team?" Bem asked.

"You are stronger," Tod said. "I don't know exactly how, but you are."

Bem was no longer able to deny it. "Somehow I have gained. I don't know why or how."

"We need you here," Sibling said. "When the heavier storms come, I will be swept away, and the pattern will be lost. Only you can preserve it. You must stay."

Bem made a flashing sigh. "I must stay," it agreed. "I will depart now, for I have another obligation, but will return to do my duty here."

"That is good," Sibling agreed.

Bem returned to the trail and resumed toboggan form so the others could ride. "I wish I could remain in the Amoeba," it said. "And with the team. I have come to appreciate your qualities and desire your friendship. But now I know I must not."

They traveled back along the trail. "We can remain friends," Tod said. "Just not together. Maybe you can visit on occasion."

"That may not be feasible," Wizard said. "When Bem departs to stay, that trail will dissipate."

"That is my expectation," Bem said. "I am experiencing

anticipatory grief."

"At least you will save your pattern," Vanja said.

"I am not sure of that. I preserved it from the minor storm, but that was enough to show me that I lack what is required to enable it to withstand the larger storms. We are doomed."

"How can you say that!" Vanja protested.

"Because it is true," Wizard said. "Scrying now, I see Bem is correct. It is not so much a defect in Bem as in the other parts of the pattern. The other participants lack the necessary resolution to survive a bad storm. They have become soft in the time since the last killer storms."

"Then the soft ones should be replaced," Veee said.

"There are no suitable replacements," Bem said. "Not in our own pattern, and qualified entities in other patterns are needed where they are."

"Then it is doom Bem is returning to!"

"Still, I must do what I can," Bem said.

"I wish we could help," Vanja said.

"It is off the trail," Wizard said. "We can't affect it."

"Bovine turds! We have already affected it, to the extent that Bem is stronger that it used to be."

"But we don't know why that is," Tod reminded her. "It may not even relate to us, but to some other aspect of the trail."

They were silent for a while, as they knew they were not getting anywhere.

"There may be one other thing we can do for you," Veee said. "We can try to solve the mystery of the manner you became better qualified than your sibling. Knowing that may further enhance your ability. It has to relate to your experience here."

"That seems likely," Bem agreed. "But I really have not

contributed significantly to the group effort."

"The hell you haven't," Tod said. "You have been supporting us all along, beginning with your prior knowledge of the android menace."

"You warmed me when I was shivering ill," Vanja said. "And Wizard, when he was depleted."

"You saved me from the wolfkeys by carrying me up the canyon wall," Veee said. "And Tod too."

"Every contribution is significant, or the group would not exist" Wizard said. "It does not need to be dramatic, merely sufficient. You carried me that last stage of the journey to the pool. Without that I could not have bombed it."

"I thank all of you for your reassurances," Bem said. "I merely did what I could at the time. You helped me too."

"The point at the moment," Veee said, "is not what Bem contributed to the effort, worthy as that was, but how Bem's participation changed it to improve its prospects in its own frame. What did Bem learn that makes a difference?"

"I love the way you zero in on relevance," Vanja said. "That *is* the question."

"I learned of the existence of the trail, and the Amoeba," Bem said as it forged up the steep slope to the intersection with the main trail. "And of the android menace, similar to ours. But it is not a renewed android invasion we now face, but storms. I doubt my experience relates."

"I wonder," Tod said. "I used to play card games on the computer—never mind what a computer is, the point is the cards. The object was to put the cards in order, but often this was difficult. Sometimes the most innocent and seemingly sensible move proved to be disastrous. You had to do something else before you made that move. Bem may have had to do something before he tackled the storms. Maybe not anything obvious, but nevertheless critical. If we can figure out what that is, then we've got it."

"This may be irrelevant," Veee said. "I noticed no humanoids in your frame, Bem, yet I think you said they exist. Where were they?"

"They exist, but do manual labors," Bem said. "They are not permitted near the fundamental pattern."

"Why not?"

"They are animals."

"Animals?"

"Non-sapient creatures, with no appreciation of art or pattern."

"Yet they resemble us, don't they?"

Bem paused. "Physically they do. But they lack intelligence. They can be trained for simple tasks, like clearing stones from a field, but that is all."

"How do you know this?"

"It is common knowledge, and has been for millennia."

"Have you ever verified this yourself, directly?"

"There was no need to verify the obvious. That would be a waste of effort."

"I wonder."

"Where are you going with this, Veee?" Tod asked.

"What Bem says about animals is true. They lack the minds to perform or appreciate art. But if these creatures look like us, they might resemble us in other ways too. Such as being smarter than animals."

"And if they are?"

"They might be able to fill in the patterns."

"Impossible," Bem said.

"Think about it," Veee said. "If we, the members of our team, could enter your realm, would be we qualified to fill those spaces?"

Again Bem considered. "Barely. You lack the ability to change colors to match the pattern shifts. But if you were placed in particular spots, such as the axles—the centers of the flowers—you would not have to change. So it is theoretically possible, because of your intelligence and application. But you are not animals."

Tod saw what Veee was driving at. "But if your humanoids did have intelligence, and were willing to participate, could they do it?"

"If and if, yes," Bem agreed. "But they don't and aren't."

Tod addressed Wizard. "Can you scry that?"

"Yes," Wizard replied after a moment. "They are smarter than Bem's folk choose to believe."

"Impossible!" Bem protested.

"In my frame this is called prejudice," Tod said. "We have thought humanoids with a different color of skin were inferior. But it turned out they weren't."

"Now I see it," Vanja said. "There are whole cultures prejudiced against vampires, calling us walking dead, confusing us with zombies, and they won't even try to get to know us."

"I would not have tried, had it not been for the facilitating ambiance of the Amoeba," Bem said. "But I am glad I came to know and appreciate you."

"And that may be the secret of your growth," Veee said. "Your expansion of tolerance. Now expand it some more, and maybe you can still save your people."

"Wizard?" Bem asked.

"My scrying indicates that this is so."

"What do you have to lose by trying it?" Tod asked. "You stand to lose anyway if you don't get some new personnel."

"I will try it," Bem said. "Your logic does not appeal, but is nevertheless persuasive. I must gamble, and this may possibly enable me to save my people."

"We sincerely hope so," Veee said.

"When it comes to prejudice, we're guilty too," Tod said. "I had no use for BEMS before I met you, or for vampires before I met Vanja, and I thought wizards were silly fiction."

"What about fifty thousand year old women?" Veee asked.

"I thought they belonged in museums. Their bones, at least." He glanced at her. "But your bones are nice enough."

"I thought it was my flesh you preferred."

"That, too. When can I have at it again?"

"Tonight, when Vanja's not looking."

"There will be some catching up to do, when I finish with Wizard," Vanja warned.

They all laughed, relaxing.

CHAPTER 9: SOURCE

They arrived back at the village. The villagers were returning to their regular life as the horror of the androids gradually faded.

"Tomorrow you'll be mended," Vanja told Wizard. "Then I'll stop harassing you and return to making Tod miserable."

"True," Wizard said a trifle wistfully. He had never had any illusion about the practical basis for her attention. But he, like Tod, now had a continuing hankering for her favors. "Then we'll go investigate your cluster of frames."

Vanja puffed up indignantly, her breasts halfway popping out of her pseudo halter. "The androids didn't come from there!"

"How do you know?"

She deflated. "I don't know. We'll investigate." She took another deep breath. "But after we prove the innocence of my frame, we'll go after yours."

"Yes, of course."

"Let's go debate in bed." She beckoned Bem. "Blanket duty."

"Not a wet one, I trust." Bem was catching on to the minor analogies of the human association.

Tod and Veee were alone together again. "I confess I am enjoying having you to myself," she murmured. "But I also miss the verve Vanja brings to it."

"Yes. I hope we can continue this relationship after the mission is accomplished."

"We can. Except for that restlessness we also share. The villagers are content to live their placid lives; we are not. That's going to be a problem."

"It is," he agreed. "It is the dream of any man to have two devoted women in his bed, as I do. But now I know that isn't enough. Not for any of us."

"Now get into me and see how long you can remain without climaxing."

He did. She kissed him repeatedly, rubbed her breasts against him, fondled his buttocks, and clenched her vagina rhythmically around his member. He tried to hold out, but in minutes his orgasm overtook him and he jetted into her. "You win," he gasped. "Again."

"I love winning," she said, kissing him once more. They were now doing it as a regular thing, both enjoying the muted competition. She always won, but he has holding out longer. She did not pretend to want continuous sex all night; she preferred to let him have it, then sleep. This was their compromise: he could have it all night if he could refrain from climaxing. The faster she made him do it, the sooner she could relax. But she did like his closeness, and did sometimes kiss him in the night.

In the morning the party headed uptrail to Vanja's intersection. Soon enough they stood at the end of her trail and gazed out at her frame.

It was impressive. Tod was surprised to discover that it was a water world, a vast ocean extending to the horizon. But of course Vanja liked to swim and sport in the water. From that sea projected extremely tall thin round towers. They reached into the sky like monstrous straws, buttressed every so often by curving connections, so that on the larger scale they formed a lattice. Evidently they did not have storms of the kind seen in Bem's frame, for this delicate skeleton of connections could not be expected to withstand even a moderate tempest.

"I will go to my abode to fetch an item," Vanja said. "With luck they will not spy me. I will sniff for android stink, and let you know."

"An item?" Tod asked.

"A breeding kit."

"A what?" Veee asked, startled.

"We vampires are a crossbreed species. We can breed as bats or in human form, so long as we match." She smiled. "A male bat has trouble making it with a human lady, for example. But a male human vamp has no trouble having sex with a female human vamp. The problem is when he does it with a fully human woman, not a transformed bat. The sex is fine, but it doesn't take. So we can actually breed only if we have a breeding kit whose salve enables reproductive compatibility."

"You're looking to breed?" Veee asked.

"Not yet. But if I continue to associate with Tod much longer, I may elect to do it. Then I will need the kit."

"But I want to breed with him!"

"And you can. You are fully human. You need no kit."

"But if you do—"

"Then our offspring will be half-siblings. You have a problem?"

Veee considered. "No."

"And I presume I have no say in this matter either," Tod said.

"Of course you do," Vanja said. "You can stop having sex with us."

Tod decided not to pursue the subject. He was fascinated and somewhat chagrined to realize that Vanja was considering him for fatherhood. He had thought she meant to move on, once she had better prospects elsewhere. That might still be the case. But now she was enlarging her options. However, it might be academic, as there was no breeding on the trail unless the Amoeba allowed it.

"The Amoeba will connect us to you as it did to Bem," Wizard said. "But try not to get in trouble, as we will not be able to rescue you only to advise you."

"I will try," Vanja agreed. "But trouble is a vampire's middle name." She approached Tod. "In case there is trouble, this to remember me by." She wrapped her arms about him and fervently kissed him. She was a passionate creature, so this was in character, but he had the impression there was more to it this time. She really did like him.

Then she transformed, and he found himself kissing the bat as it hovered in air. She just couldn't resist.

The bat flew out from the trail and into the water world, staying close to the surface. It dodged around the towers and soon was lost to direct physical view. But Tod could still see it via the Amoeba sight, like a camera flying beside it.

Other bats were flying to and from the towers. They ignored Vanja, or seemed to. That was surely best, if she was effectively banished from her home group. If the rival female got wind of her return, there would be mischief.

"I smell no android," Vanja said. She actually spoke in a bat cheep, but they heard it in words. Tod was impressed again with the powers of the Amoeba. They were still discovering its capacities.

"That is good," Wizard replied. "You don't have to go inside."

"Yes I do."

Soon Vanja circled a tower, climbing to the top. Tod realized that Vanja's abode was likely to be close to the terminus of the trail, because the Amoeba would have sought her, as it had Tod and the others.

At the top of the tower was a small aperture. The bat dived into it, entering a dark tube large enough only for a flying bat. Tod appreciated how that could be a significant protection, because neither sea predators nor air predators of any size could navigate it. Somehow they were able to see, though there was no light.

The bat dropped down inside the tower, diving at a swift pace. Down, down, impossibly far. Then Tod realized that the tower went below the water, and that was where Vanja was going.

The bat came to a nexus, a globular joining of a number of tunnels leading to caves. Other bats were here. There was a cheep; one of them recognized her. That could be bad news.

Vanja zoomed for a particular cave. She swooped in, picked up an object, and swooped back out to the juncture.

But now several more bats were there. They flew up before her, blocking her way. Trouble indeed.

"Let me go," Vanja cheeped. "I will not return."

"That's what you said before. Now you must die."

Vanja arrowed directly for them, knocking a hole in their formation, and zoomed back up the tower corridor. They reorganized and pursued, but were unable to catch her. The shaft was not wide enough for them to overtake her, so they were limited.

Then more bats appeared above, sealing off the exit. There was no room to maneuver. She was trapped.

"I'm doomed," she squeaked. "I love you, Veee. You too, Tod.

Now I will die fighting."

"Transform!" Tod cried.

She hovered between the bats above and below. "I can't do that here! There's not room. We're conditioned."

"The Amoeba can enable it," Tod said. "Try!"

Vanja hesitated. "What the hell. I'll die anyway. Might as well go out with a bang."

She exploded into human form. It was way too big for the narrow column. The tower burst apart and collapsed; it was evidently constructed to withstand pressure from outside, not inside. Water surged in. The other bats squeaked with horror as they were immersed. Then they too transformed, becoming naked male and female humans.

Veee banged him on the shoulder. Tod realized he was staring at the females, all of whom were well formed and healthy, like Vanja. Veee wasn't jealous, merely letting him know she knew. He put a hand on her bottom and squeezed reassuringly.

Vanja stroked upward. Others pursued her, but she had the advantage of surprise and a head start. She reached the surface, transformed again, and flew into the air. The others followed, but she maintained her lead as she fled toward the trail.

She made it. The others collected around the terminus, baffled; Vanja seemed to have disappeared into air.

Vanja came up to Tod. She still carried the little kit, its string in her mouth, hooked around a fang. She flung her arms about him, and dissolved into sobbing.

What could he do but hold her? He released Veee's buttock and embraced Vanja. "We love you too," he murmured in her ear.

She began to recover her poise. "Did I say that? I thought I was going to die."

"We'll keep your secret," Veee said, smiling.

Vanja turned Tod loose and embraced Veee. At this point Tod wasn't certain which of them Vanja liked better.

"What possessed you to go in there?" Wizard demanded. "You had already ascertained that the androids did not come from your frame."

"If you'd bothered to scry, you'd have known. I had to get the kit." She unhooked it from her tooth and efficiently bound it into her hair, out of sight.

"You are crazy."

"Thank you."

"You're batty in your belfry," Tod said.

"For wanting you," Vanja agreed.

"The entire courtship routine seems somewhat insane to me," Bem said.

"Thank you," Vanja said again. Then they all laughed.

They returned to the village. "Now it seems to be my turn," Wizard said. "This should be routine, but won't be."

"Something will go wrong?" Vanja asked.

"My scrying indicates that Gianna is watching. The moment I leave the trail, she will intercept me."

"A woman!" Vanja said, smiling. "That's surely mischief."

"There are details about my frame I may have neglected to mention before. It is governed by the giants. We normal sized people do their bidding lest we annoy them and get stepped on, literally. Because my abilities are valuable, I had no trouble, and they catered to my lifestyle. But when they sought to remove me from retirement—well, that was when the trail sought me, and I took it. I thought that would be the end of it. But if I must return, however briefly, I may have difficulty extricating myself from Gianna's embrace."

"Now this is getting more interesting," Vanja said. "Your wife died, but there's another woman?"

"A giant?" Veee asked, also intrigued. "How big is she?"

"The giants are about ten times the height of normal folk, and a thousand times the mass."

"They must be made of squeezed lead!"

"No, it's the normal square cube ratio," Tod said. "If the proportions are similar. Ten times the height, ten times the width, ten times the depth. Ten cubed, or a thousand."

Vanja looked at Veee. "Does this make sense to you?"

Veee concentrated, working out the concept. "Yes, I think it does. But it must require magic to prevent them from having elephant legs." She had learned about elephants from Tod, who had confirmed what had become legends in her tribe.

"So if such a creature treads on you," Bem said, "The pressure is quite strong."

"It is," Wizard agreed. "I might fend such an action off briefly with my magic, but then they would have gone after my family. As a general rule, one does not say no to a giant."

"Yet you were not satisfied to continue serving," Bem said. "Was the duty onerous?"

"Not at all. They used me mainly for scrying difficult situations. I enjoyed the work."

"Then it must have been something about Gianna," Vanja said.

"Yes. After my wife died, Gianna took a more personal interest in me. At first I thought she was merely ensuring that I would scry well. Then I scried her, and learned that she was intrigued by me personally, despite my age and size. It seems she has an obscure hankering for novelty."

"She wants to have sex with you!" Vanja exclaimed, delighted. "Ten times your size! That's novelty all right."

"Novelty," Wizard agreed wanly.

"Is that possible?" Veee asked. "Your whole body would fit inside her, well—"

"It is a talent of giants to revert to the size of their ancestors, for a while," Wizard said. "For long enough. So that aspect is feasible."

"Afraid you won't perform?" Vanja asked. "Is she ugly?"

"No, she's beautiful. "That's how she achieved power among the giants: by seducing any male who challenged her."

Vanja nodded, unsurprised. "Will she demand disgusting things, like coitus interruptus or kissing her dirty toes?"

Tod kept his amusement to himself. Ejaculation into any female orifice was fine with the vampire, but doing it on the ground was an offensive waste. Similarly it was the dirt, not the portion of the body, that bothered her. Vanja was scrupulously clean.

"No, she likes it the old fashioned way."

"Then what's the problem?"

"She will want me to scry things I prefer not to. It's a matter of professional ethics."

"And if you tell her no?"

"She'll seduce me until I can't deny her. She'll corrupt me. Then her will will be mine."

"Well, of course," Vanja said. "It's a woman's way."

"And then when I am of no further use to her, having done her dirty work, and advancing age diminishes my magical powers, she'll step on me."

"And that's a ruler's way," Tod said.

"Point finally made," Vanja said. "You can't go home."

"But I can't verify the android presence without stepping into my frame, however briefly."

"You're the strategist, Tod," Veee said. "Tell him how to navigate that challenge."

"I don't think I can do that."

"Do it, or I'll seduce you and then step on you," Vanja said. "With my dirty toes."

That actually gave Tod a notion. "Maybe there is a way. She will catch you right at the edge of the trail?"

"She can't see the trail, but she knows where I disappeared, and therefore where I must reappear, and when. She has had a lesser scryer identify the place and time. She will be right there."

"You can't poke your head out, sniff for androids, and pull back?"

"She will catch me and push me away, blocking the access so I can't return."

"Then you must welcome her embrace," Tod said.

"That is folly!"

"No. Let me explain." Tod explained. Veee, Vanja, and Bem agreed with his logic.

Wizard sighed. "My scrying agrees too. I shall have to do it, albeit it with misgivings."

"Misgivings?" Vanja asked. "Consider sex with her a peripheral benefit."

"I don't like lying."

She looked at him cannily. "Is it really lying? You have had a hankering for her all along, haven't you?"

"I was married!"

"And now you're free." She fixed him with a challenging stare. "Admit it: the reason I was able to seduce you was that in a small way I resembled her. You pretended I was her."

Tod saw the Wizard's look of dismay that indicated she had scored. Vanja tended to do that when she focused. "But will she believe it? She is a woman scorned."

"She'll believe what her vanity chooses to believe. Women can be utter fools when their pride is in question."

Tod saw Veee nod.

Wizard shifted the subject. "My scrying does not guarantee success, it merely indicates that it is feasible provided I don't, as you phrase it, screw up."

"Screw her, not up," Vanja agreed. "Better go naked, so as to be sure there's no impediment."

"You are merciless."

"I'm a cynical woman like your giantess. I know how you must handle that type."

"I will not go naked. I must seem not to be expecting her. So she thinks she has caught me unaware."

"Good point," Vanja agreed reluctantly. "She has to believe she has outsmarted you. That will make her overconfident."

Veee nodded again. Women naturally understood female psychology. "But let your robe accidentally fall open when your member stirs, so she knows she is arousing you."

"Flash her," Vanja agreed.

"It is good to have such competent instruction," Wizard said dourly. Both women smiled.

They went to the end of the trail. Tod saw a modest living chamber with a bed, desk, and clothing rack. But no giantess. "Maybe she's not watching right now," he said.

"She is there, merely masked by the illusion of invisibility. Minor magic via a canned spell so she doesn't have to show her nakedness to lowly personnel who don't deserve to see it."

"I am almost getting to like this woman," Vanja said. "She has good instincts."

"Do not try to emulate her," Wizard warned. "You are similarly cynical, but she has depths of viciousness you lack."

"Maybe I merely conceal them better."

"No."

Vanja shrugged, not displeased, and kissed him. "Get going, lover."

Wizard adjusted his robe, for the moment opening it so his torso showed, practicing the maneuver. His body was old and frail, unsurprising at his age.

"And get it up when you see her," Vanja reminded him. "Can you do that?"

"I'm not sure. She looks like a lovely woman, enhanced as she is by illusion, but I know her awful power and unscrupulous nature. That is daunting."

"I'd better help you. Will you accept?"

Wizard glanced down as if appreciating his unaroused state and sighed. "Perhaps I should."

So she had bitten him before, to facilitate his potency. That explained that aspect.

Vanja bent her head down and grazed his throat with a fang. "That's minimal; it will last you about fifteen minutes. Do it before it expires."

Wizard looked down again, as if his member were stirring. She had delivered a drop of potency potion.

"Thank you." He stepped through. "No android odor," he murmured.

"Aha!"

Wizard turned to see Gianna, nude, standing between him and the trail terminus. The rest of them saw her too, now that she had doffed her invisibility. She must have stood behind the terminus, let him pass, then stepped forward to block his return. It was smart management.

Apart from that, she was one stunningly beautiful nude woman. Her proportions were spectacular, like Vanja's only more pronounced; her face was innocently lovely; her hair was a serpentine coil around her torso that managed to enhance rather than conceal anything of interest. Even her feet were sculptured marvels with no dirt at all. A man could kiss them with no shame. Many surely had.

Vanja knocked Tod's his shoulder, much as Veee had before. "You're appreciating her too much, jerk."

Tod put his left arm around her and closed his hand on her left breast. "Fortunately I can't touch her."

"That's better." She took a deep breath so that her breast pressed against his fingers.

Veee came to his other side and set his right arm around and on her similarly. "That stiffness you're getting had better be for us," she murmured.

"Fascinating ritual," Bem said.

"Oh, shut up, or we'll start putting our meat against you," Vanja said.

Bem was amused but silent.

"I'm so glad to see you," Wizard said insincerely to Gianna.

"Really? And so you hid from me?"

"You have tempted me for years. My wife would not have understood."

"You bet! And if I'd taken you, she would have suicided and you would have blamed me, of all things, and been virtually useless thereafter. So I let you be; you were too useful to dispense with at the time."

"I appreciate your discretion." The irony was deliberately naked. They were playing a high-stakes game.

"However, you did not come to me after she died. Instead you vanished into whatever magical hinterland you have access to. You were avoiding me. What paltry excuse do you proffer?"

"Would you believe I was in mourning?"

"Only with difficulty."

"Nevertheless, I needed time." Wizard took a deep breath, preparing to speak the big lie. "I took that time. Then I realized that I craved your company."

She laughed. "Try again, liar. You know what a huge bitch I am."

Wizard let his robe fall open, flashing her. "I was attempting to be discreet. Your personality is as big a horror as your natural size. But your body—that is what I crave." Now his member was rising, thanks to Vanja's injection. "I want to plumb it before I die, just as I dreamed of doing all those years."

"Now that is more like it," Gianna said approvingly. "Realistic desperation. And you shall have it. Of course you know there is a price."

"I prefer not to pay that price."

"As if you have a choice. First you must scry for me; then I will reward you in my fashion."

Wizard's member was now almost fully erect. "I can't wait. I must have you now." He advanced on her.

Gianna eyed the member, intrigued. "That's a better elevation than you got for your wife." Which hinted how closely she had been observing him.

"You're a sexier bitch than my wife ever was." He threw his arms around her.

She could readily have thrown him back, but yielded to his urgency. "I'm flattered. Maybe this once, then the scrying before you get any more. Kiss me."

He thrust his face at her as he thrust his groin at hers, pushing her back. Pleased, she used a hand to make sure of his placement, then let herself sink backward as he entered. It was obvious she had control, and liked catering to his desperate need. She knew that he knew she was a vicious bitch, yet couldn't help himself, overpowered by her sexual allure. The girls were right: women could be as great fools as men, when their vanity was on the line.

And as the penetration progressed, Wizard passed the threshold and got on the trail.

Gianna was left lying on her back, naked, empty, legs spread, arms clasping nothing. The prey had escaped.

"DAMN! *DAMN!* **DAMN!**" she swore, catching on immediately. Her body exploded into its natural size, tenfold in every direction.

"Wow," Tod murmured as Vanja and Veee went to help Wizard to his feet. For the giantess remained visible, her body occupying the space where they stood, overlapping them like an illusion. In fact Tod himself was standing where her monstrous lifted thighs came down to expose her giant cleft; he was chest deep in it. Indeed, a whole man would fit inside there, if properly angled. She might even have used men that way, for novelty or punishment.

Then Gianna sat up, her breasts swinging over Tod's head like gargantuan wrecking balls, and lurched to her feet. She was way too big for the chamber, which burst around her much as the thin tower had when Vanja transformed. But she wasn't satisfied. She squatted, providing Tod another compelling view of her elephantine flexing juncture, and used her immense fists to pulverize what remained of Wizard's abode. Then she stood again and stomped the fragments into splinters. Tod was now standing directly under her, looking up, absolutely fascinated by the scene as she lifted one leg, then the other, and made her flesh rock with each impact.

"Hell hath no fury..." he murmured.

"Better quit before your eyes pop out of their sockets," Vanja said.

"Or something else does," Veee added.

Tod realized that his erection was straining to break out of his trousers. He simply had never before seen such a display, so close and active.

"Shame to waste two such fine erections," Vanja said, glancing at both men. "Why don't we pause to— "

"This is too close to the edge," Veee demurred. "Someone might roll back off the trail and be caught by fury incarnate."

"You're too damned practical," Vanja said. "But also right, unfortunately."

The girls hustled Tod and Wizard back along the trail, each man bemused in his own fashion.

"Fascinating demonstration," Bem remarked. "The woman's concluding anatomy was impressive."

They had to laugh.

"There was no odor of android there," Wizard said. "We have eliminated three prospects."

"Then it must be my turn," Veee said.

"Are you ready for a similar experience?" Bem asked.

"No. But my frame should be relatively quiet. It's the most primitive one. The day is not done. I want to get this over with."

They went back along the trail Veee and Tod had come along. Now Tod saw Veee's home frame, a lightly forested region. That was likely the Middle East, as it was 50,000 years ago, in a temperate period.

"If there is mischief," Vanja warned Veee, "come right back to the trail. We don't want to lose you."

Veee kissed her and stepped out. "I do not smell android," she announced.

"Where did you come from, Veee?" a man's voice asked. He was a tall, muscular man, not unhandsome, wearing a kind of breechclout.

Veee whirled. "Hooo!" she exclaimed, recognizing him.

"I was coming to take a poop, and suddenly you appeared. Where have you been these past few days? Where were you hiding?"

"I was tacitly banished because of that sand painting I made," she reminded him. "So I had to look for some other tribe that might want me."

"Oh, yes. You had no business messing with sand. But how did you appear out of nothing just now?"

"Maybe you weren't paying attention."

"I'm a hunter! I always pay attention. You appeared like a spook." His eyes narrowed with suspicion. "Have you become a ghost?"

"No, of course not!"

"I'll find out," he moved suddenly, and caught her arm. "You have flesh. But I'd better make sure you're there inside too. You could be an empty shell." He drew her to him, fiddling with his clout to expose his rising member.

"No!"

Hooo paused. "What?"

"Women don't tell men no, in her culture," Tod explained to the others. "Rape is unknown, because the women have only the option to accede to the man's will."

"I don't want to do it," Veee said. "Let me go."

Hooo's brow furrowed. "Don't want to do what?"

"Don't want to have sex with you. I'm my own woman now."

He stared at her. "You are a spook! Well, I'll cure that soon enough." He held her close, guiding his turgid member under her cloak.

Veee swung her free arm, smacking him on the side of the head with her fist. Startled, he let her go. She whirled and ran. After a moment he pursued. Now he was angry.

Veee ran for the trail. But Hooo tackled her and brought her down to the ground, prone. Then he hiked up her robe to bare her bottom and readied his member again. Sex was on his mind, and he meant to have it.

"Get on your hands and knees," Tod called, knowing Veee could hear him while the man could not.

"That will just make it easier for him," Veee gasped.

"You won't stay there," Tod told her. "Do it."

Veee humped her strong body, getting her rear up, then her shoulders. "Ah, now you are cooperating, as you should," Hooo said, pulling her bottom in to him.

"Now race forward, hands and knees," Tod said.

Veee did. Surprised, Hooo pursued her awkwardly on his knees.

"Now get to your feet, turn into him and pick him up," Tod said. "Carry him to the trail."

Veee smiled. She followed directions, and in moments had Hooo draped across her sturdy shoulders, too amazed to resist. Her actions had been totally unexpected.

She carried him to the nearby trail—and vanished as she entered, just as Wizard had. Hooo dropped to the ground, clearly confused.

Veee saw that she was free, and collapsed herself. Vanja leaped to catch her, and held her close. "It's okay to cry," she said. "You could have been raped and killed."

Veee cried. Tod and Wizard, embarrassed, turned away. It was clear that the two women were now firm friends, and understood each other in ways the men did not.

"This too is interesting," Bem said.

"I guess the prospect of rape is worse to a woman than to a man," Tod said.

"No it isn't," Vanja called. "Just think about being involuntarily sodomized by a brute ogre, and you'll get it."

Tod and Wizard shared a shudder. "We get it," Tod said.

"But you did help," Vanja said. "Come here."

Tod went to them. Veee transferred to him, all damp and grateful. "Thank you! I couldn't think what to do."

"I was able to be more objective, because I wasn't the one under attack," Tod said.

She drew her face back a bit, gazing into his eyes. "If he had done it, would you still want me?"

That was her concern? "Yes! I love you."

He felt her tension dissipating. "I learned to be my own woman, from you. I couldn't stand to return to the old way. If I'd just let him do it, then he would have finished and gone away. But I was afraid I would lose you."

"No, Veee no! You had a right to fight back."

They paused to watch Hooo, who was bewilderedly getting to his feet. Now he was sure he had encountered a ghost. After a moment he walked away, shaking his head.

"I'd have knifed him," Vanja said.

"I never thought of my knife!" Veee said, chagrined.

"Neither did we," Vanja said. "But maybe it's better to let him go tell his story. It might make tribesmen more cautious about raping women, for fear you will reappear and carry them away."

Veee smiled. "Yes." She swallowed. "I can't go back."

"Neither can I," Vanja said. "Or Wizard. All of us really understand that now."

"I could," Tod said. "But I don't want to. There's nothing for me there."

"Except to sniff out the androids," Vanja said. "If they're not near your frame, it's going to be a more complicated search."

"There's still time today," Tod said. "Let's do it."

They backtracked along Veee's trail, intersected Tod's, and went to his terminus. There was his house, unchanged.

He stepped off the trail. He sniffed the air, expecting it to be clean.

And caught a faint whiff of android. Oh, no!

He stopped back on the trail. "I smelled it. Faint, but there. It could have been there before, and I didn't catch it, but now I'm sensitized to it."

"That means the android trail is close to this one," Wizard said.

"But not on this one," Tod said. "How do we get at it?"

"We sniff it out," Vanja said. "The traces are probably there; we just missed them."

"Yes," Wizard said. "We were not really alert until Tod verified its presence. This suggests that there is no active contact, merely the potential for it. Which in turn means we are on time. If we cut off this trail, the menace will be abated."

They backtracked. They had taken no more than ten steps when Veee sniffed and announced it. "Here."

They were in the forest, before the trees became alien. There was an overgrown offshoot none of them had noticed on the way out. "Here," Vanja agreed, sniffing.

Bem forged along it like a small tank, flattening it for the others. Soon they were at the terminus.

"But can I go there?" Tod asked. "When it's not exactly my frame?"

"You should be able to go there partially," Wizard said. "This seems to be so close to yours that it should be almost complete for you."

Tod wasn't sure what that meant, but decided to risk it. He stepped out and sniffed the air.

The odor of android was much stronger. This was the place.

He stepped back onto the trail. "This is it. It looks like my frame, only a different location."

"It is your near future," Wizard said. "I was able to scry that much."

"My near future? Won't that put me into paradox?"

"You will not be able to. Paradox is self limiting."

Tod hoped Wizard was correct. "So what should I do?"

"Go out there and locate the source. Learn what you can of it, especially the identity of the one who took this trail. Get me that, and I can scry the rest."

"How can I learn that? It could be anyone in this world."

Wizard considered. "No. The trail must terminate near the person's residence. Check for that."

Tod, dubious, went out again. There was a yard, and a house, similar to those he knew. He walked up to the door and tried the handle.

His hand passed through the knob. He was a ghost, as Veee had been. So this was not that close to his own frame.

Well, in that case...

He walked through the door into the house. It seemed to be deserted. Not surprising, since its proprietor had taken the trail. Tod made his way to the bedroom—fortunately it was a ground level residence, with no upper story—and looked at the dresser. There was a picture of a young man with a young woman. A married couple? One took the trail? Then where was the other?

"Wizard, can you scry this picture?" Tod asked.

"Yes. That is a married couple. The man works at the plasma factory. His wife Hellene had an increasing problem with that, because the idea of creating life in the laboratory conflicts which her religion. She finally left him. He, disconsolate, took the trail. He took one sample android with him and set it loose, hoping it would find a home in the wilderness."

"There's our source!" Tod exclaimed.

"Yes. You don't need to check the factory; we have what we need. Come back in before there is mischief."

Tod was glad to comply. He walked back through the closed door and toward the trail. It was a relief to make it safely back, though there had not been any immediate threat he was aware of. He was almost disappointed.

But just as his foot came to the portal, something happened. He was lifted into the air. "What?"

"Something has caught you in an electronic net," Bem said. "It appears to be a trap set to spring when you approach this point."

"Why didn't it spring when I came into this world?" Tod asked, floundering around in an effort to gain purchase on something.

"Probably your first passage primed it, and your second set it off," Bem said. "We have such traps in my frame. They are used to capture marauding animals. Normal animals pass by and do not return; marauders linger to do their damage."

"How do I get out of this?"

"You must wait until the trap proprietor comes to free you."

"Great," Tod muttered. His routine visit had abruptly become un-routine.

"Here they come now," Vanja said.

It appeared to be a garden tractor with two men riding it. It was floating over the landscape. There was no loud motor or blast of air; it simply moved along without support.

"Levitation," Wizard said, sounding impressed.

"Or anti-gravity," Tod said, also impressed. "This is a future realm."

The tractor nosed up to where Tod was suspended. "What is it, Dib?" one man asked.

"An invisible spook, Dab" the other said. "Seems we caught one."

Tod was startled by the fact that he could understand them, in contrast to his experience with Veee when she left the trail. Then he realized why: this was his own near future. The language had not changed, just the technology.

"But it was Bison we were looking for, not a ghost. What's a ghost doing here?"

"Maybe Bison died?"

"There was never a life-terminus indication," Dib said. "He just vanished without explanation."

"Leaving his wife distraught. She thinks it's her fault."

"Well, Hellene had left him," Dib said. "That really broke him up. He might have done something."

"He did," Dab said. "But I don't think he died."

"Well, we'd better take this spook to the incinerator at the Gunk Works and reset the trap. Maybe the next catch won't be a false alarm."

"The incinerator!" Tod exclaimed. "I don't like the sound of that."

"When a trap catches something supernatural, incineration is normally the preferred way to abolish it," Bem said.

"I'm so glad for that explanation!"

Now the tractor was floating rapidly over the town, Tod in tow. Soon it reached a steeply walled enclosure. Tod could see faint smoke rising from what looked like a giant oven. "If you have anything in mind, better make it quick," he said, trying to sound more assured than he felt.

"They must release you in order to put you in the incinerator," Bem said. "They won't want to burn up a good trap. The moment they do that, zoom rapidly toward the trail."

"Zoom? How do I do that?"

"The trail attracts you," Wizard said. "In your present state of dissipation, that attraction should be enough to draw you to it. Go with the flow."

"I'll try," Tod said. He had a sick premonition that this was to be his ignominious end.

The tractor halted at the incinerator. There was a large intake hopper. Air started whooshing in, like a vacuum cleaner.

The force field holding Tod clicked off. He started floating toward the hopper, about to be sucked in.

"Now!" Bem said.

Tod leaped back the way they had come, somehow bracing against the air. He grabbed the edge of the tractor and hauled himself over and past it, his hands sinking into it but gaining some slight purchase. He sailed into the air. Then something drew on him, and he picked up speed, floating toward the trail.

He was escaping, and Dib and Dab never missed him. He was an invisible spook. He sailed onward over the houses and gardens of the town, picking up speed.

He reached the trail terminus, and this time there was no trap. Safe!

"What now?" he asked with fake bravado as he crossed the threshold and the others come into view, as if materializing from nothing.

Veee caught him and drew him close, kissing him. That was exactly what he needed. He felt safe in her embrace.

Tod realized that Bem had not been doing much when the others checked their frames, but Bem had been there for Tod this time. Bem's advice had been critical. "Thanks, Bem!"

"I had thought there must be reason for my continued presence," Bem said. "I am glad to have been of service."

"Now we must locate that man Bison," Wizard said. "And

persuade him to go home, thus severing his path."

"To a disaffected wife? That may be tricky."

"Consider it a challenge," Vanja said.

"But the men indicated that Hellene may have had a change of heart," Veee said. "That should count for something."

Tod hoped so. He did not want to have to come to this future frame again. That had been too close a call.

CHAPTER 10: METASTASIS

They returned to the village to rest for the night. "Can you scry to locate Bison?" Tod asked Wizard.

"No. I need to be in contact with a person, or have a personal object before me, as I did when you saw the picture. That covered the personal history only up to the point the picture last saw the man. Where Bison went after coming here I can't fathom."

"We can ask around," Vanja said. "Some villager surely knows. He'll tell." She flashed a fang briefly.

"Suppose it's a woman?" Veee asked.

"Then Tod will have to ask her. I'm sure he can charm a woman when he really tries."

"What, without a love potion?"

"Wizard will provide him one."

They were having their fun again. "Suppose I have to make out with her?" Tod asked. "To get her to talk? Some villagers are canny bargainers."

The girls exchanged a horrified look. "That would be a problem," Veee said seriously.

"Maybe give her medicine to prevent vomiting?" Vanja suggested.

"I can make a spell for that," Wizard said.

"You too, Brutus," Tod muttered.

"Fascinating," Bem said. "You are all teasing each other, knowing that you don't mean what you say. Open duplicity that somehow enhances your appreciation of each other when it should be having the opposite effect."

"It's a bisexual thing," Vanja said.

"Sometimes I almost wish I could become male or female just long enough to fathom the nuances."

"Don't risk it," Tod said. "It would require a lifetime."

"And probably ruin you for pattern formation," Veee said.

"A horrible risk!" Bem agreed.

As it turned out, all Tod had to do was ask. Several villagers knew of Bison, who had served honorably on a recent mission, then retired to a neighboring village to farm. "He lost his home-world wife," a buxom woman explained. "He is still hurting. Won't touch any of us." She smiled, inhaling. "Yet."

Tod could see how leftover team members could get drawn into local relationships. The villagers lurked.

They walked to the other village. It turned out that Bison, distraught, had decided to suicide.

"We can't let him do that," Wizard said.

"Because the mission is not yet complete," Tod agreed. "We need him to return to his frame so the trail will close off."

"Won't it shut down when he dies?" Veee asked.

That made all of them pause. "Maybe we should just leave him alone," Vanja said.

"Scry it," Bem suggested.

Wizard did. "That will not complete our mission," he announced. "It would be a losing ploy."

"I'm relieved," Veee said. "We'd be guilty of murder. But why does he need to live?"

They considered it as they set out to follow Bison's route, Bem seining for the traces the man had left as he moved.

"If his trail shuts down whether he leaves or dies," Vanja said, "what else can there be that relates to our mission?"

They passed it back and fourth, but were unable to come up with an answer.

"I am reminded of computerized card games," Tod said. "In my boredom I have played many games of Klondike, Baker's Dozen, and Free Cell, mainly. There is a program that signals the state of each game as Winnable, Unwinnable, Undetermined, Won, or Lost. I learned to watch that, and the moment it stopped saying Winnable, I backed off and tried another route. That enabled me to win almost every time. But sometimes it was like getting into a swamp. The program didn't tell me what move to make, merely whether I could win. In effect it blocked out my wrong moves without clueing me in on the right ones. I could try everything, and nothing lead to victory. Yet I know there had to be a way. So I just kept plugging along until finally, mainly by trial and error I found the key and then went on to win. But here's the thing: sometimes the obvious move was a loser regardless how it looked for immediate gain, and sometimes the right move seemed pointless, until it led deviously to a breakthrough. The Amoeba seems like that. We don't understand why letting Bison die is the wrong move, but it is, and we need to find the right move."

"Interesting analysis," Bem said. "The Amoeba is silent, yet we are sufficiently attuned to it to know whether we are properly pursuing our mission. How does your Winnable adviser know the correct route?"

"I've never been sure of that. I assume it is like running water through a blocked sieve to locate the one or two open channels. When the last one is closed off, the program knows. It is not intelligent, merely tracking."

"As seems to be the case with the Amoeba," Wizard agreed. "From the time it summons us until we complete the mission, it is watching, informing us when we go wrong."

"Maybe, because it spans time as well as space, it can see the future," Veee said. "So it knows when something goes wrong. All it can do is alert us."

Vanja transformed and flew silently ahead.

"How did the Amoeba come about?" Tod asked. "I know programmers set up the Winnable program, but who set up the Amoeba?"

"Are you religious?"

"Not really."

"Then you won't accept that God did it."

"I won't," Tod agreed.

"Or that the Amoeba is God."

Tod whistled. "I rather doubt that God exists, but I'm pretty sure the Amoeba exists. I'm not sure I want to set it up as God, though."

"I think of it as an entity that evolved to fill a need, and the need is to keep some sort of order in an otherwise chaotic universe or complex of universes. It doesn't have to be a deity."

The bat returned, becoming the woman. "I spy Bison," Vanja said. "He is approaching the brink of a chasm. We are closer to the gulf than the top; I doubt we can reach him in time to stop him from jumping."

"Can you levitate him safely down if he jumps?" Veee asked Wizard.

"Not from this distance. An with the scrying, I have to be close to my subject."

Tod took over. "Vanja, fly up there and try to tempt him into tarrying. Bem, get below him in the chasm and form a pneumatic mat to break his fall without harming him. Wizard, cast an illusion to make Bem's location seem like the deepest, darkest depth of the chasm. That is, the best place to jump if you're serious about suicide. Veee, you and I will be the decoy party hurrying toward him to remonstrate. Our approach may make him jump, but we're ready for that."

"We hope," Veee said.

Vanja flew and Bem formed into a ball and rolled bouncingly into the chasm before them. Tod and Veee forged up the path Bison had taken. Tod wasn't sure he had made the best plan, but speed was of the essence.

They saw the bat glide down toward the standing man and become the woman. She would be telling him her nature, and asking him to tarry with her a while before making his decision. She would be showing her voluptuosity. She just might be able to satisfy him that life still had something to offer.

She took a step toward him, arms widespread.

Bison turned and leaped. He plunged down toward the depth of the chasm.

"Damn!" Tod said. The delay had not been long enough to be sure Bem was in place.

Then they saw the man sail back up out of the void. Bem had made it, and caught the man in a trampoline type net. Soon he would bounce to a safe landing. They had done it.

Vanja flew down to rejoin the man, and the others hurried to join her. Before long they converged on a somewhat disconcerted would-be suicide.

"Your vampire friend has explained it," Bison called as they approached. "You folk want me alive. Why?"

"We are a team summoned by the Amoeba," Tod said. "Just as you were, before. We don't know ourselves why you need to be alive, but it seems you do. Our mission is not complete until we relate to you. You know how the Amoeba is." This was an educated guess.

"I know," Bison agreed. "But I have sinned against the Amoeba. I deserve to die."

Sinned? Tod kept his attitude carefully neutral, suspecting he knew the answer. "How so?"

"I completed my mission. Then I—I fetched the android. The one you folk just had to deal with. But for you, it would have wiped out this semi-paradise the Amoeba has made along the trail. As it was, it was one hell of a siege, and many innocent people died. I can't make it up to them or to you. I deserve to die. Now you know."

There it was, confirming Wizard's scrying. "Why did you fetch the android?"

"They were going to destroy the whole batch, there at the gunk works. I recognized it as a significant new kind of life. I wanted to give it its chance." Bison shook his head. "I was an utter fool."

"Men often are," Vanja said. "But usually about women, rather than androids."

Bison smiled briefly. Evidently she had made an impression on him, unsurprisingly. "It's an ethical thing. I did not realize how vicious that creation was. I guess I was blinded by ideology. I wish I had listened to my wife." He shook his head. "And that's the rest of why I need to die. I don't really want to live without her."

"Hellene," Vanja said.

Bison looked at her, startled. "What do you know of Hellene?"

Vanja glanced at Todd, but he merely nodded, letting her take it, as Bison seemed receptive to her.

"We checked your frame," she said. "We learned that Hellene left you because she had to, when she saw you going wrong. She still loves you, Bison." She was going beyond what they knew; it was what they needed the situation to be, to get the man to go home.

Bison seemed to sink into pained nostalgia. "Ooh, Hellene!" he murmured. "You were so right."

"Go to her," Vanja urged. "She needs you."

"Why would she believe I've changed?"

"Because you have changed. Tell her that. Apologize, abase yourself, beg her to give you another chance. She'll believe you because she wants to, and it's true. Then you can make sure no other androids ever get loose from the gunk works. That's how you will make up for what you have done."

Hope dawned. "You think?"

"I know."

"I took the trail because I had no further reason to stay, without Hellene. Even before the android."

"We all came here for similar reasons," Vanja said. "Now you no longer need the trail."

"Damn it, I'll do it!"

"We'll escort you home," Vanja said, blowing him a kiss.

Tod nodded with admiration. Vanja was good. She was making sure Bison didn't change his mind before leaving.

They walked as a group back toward the village. "How did you stop it?" Bison asked.

"We magically bombed it," Wizard replied.

Bison looked at him. "You're a wizard!"

"He does illusion, scrying, fire-starting, and telekinesis," Vanja said. "As well as the magic bomb."

"I do," Wizard said. "It seemed that my magic was required for this mission, so the Amoeba summoned me. It has been an experience."

"I know how that is. I'm a technical engineer, but it turned out my skills were required in a primitive manner. Not that the Amoeba cares if you're overqualified, just that you can fill the slot it needs at the moment. Your other traits are peripheral. But I think you did it the hard way, if you can do electronic magic like fire starting."

Now Wizard was really interested. "There was an easier way?"

"The android was designed to be readily nullified, just in case things went wrong. The pool communicates with its minions via an electronic signal that can be nulled simply by changing one bit. So all you had to do was reach out magically and change that bit, or even generate the illusion of change, so that the pool could no longer communicate with its minions. Then the crabs would drop dead, and the pool would slowly starve, no danger to any creature that did not carelessly fall into it."

"I could have done that," Wizard agreed ruefully. "Instead we put all of us at risk invading the pool."

"How could you know? The Amoeba doesn't tell you how, just what."

"We blocked the signal with my poncho," Tod said.

"It probably changed the signal just enough to make it unreadable," Bison said. "As I said, this thing was designed to be easy to stop. My folly was in not realizing that in a non-technological setting without my signal modifier, there would be no stopping it. It became monstrous. Like an invasive predator that wipes out all the local rabbits, then goes on to other animals, like people. I had not thought to bring a signal modifier, so I could not stop what I had started. All I could do was pretend to ignore it, hoping it would crash on its own, the more fool I."

Vanja patted his hand. "We all make mistakes."

Bison glanced at her. "If you were not so devastatingly beautiful, I would dismiss that as ignorant."

She smiled. "Maybe that's why I was summoned. To make ignorance seem worthwhile."

"To think I thought vampires were cold blooded demons."

"There are different types. I'm not cold."

Tod exchanged a quick glance with Veee. The vampire had not refuted one part of the charge, probably deliberately.

They reached the village, where they nighted. The team camped outside it, except for Vanja, who remained with Bison, doing her bit to cheer him and keep him on track and to remind him of the kind of welcome Hellene surely would give him.

"She is becoming a good person," Veee remarked as she hugged Tod. "She says she tried it at first as a role to get along with us, but is coming to like being a nice girl."

"Isn't she?"

"Nice? No, she's utterly cynical. But the longer she plays the nice role, the better she gets at it. That can be useful, as we are seeing with Bison. I could never charm him like that."

"You are charming me well enough."

"Thank you." She wrapped her legs about him and continued from there. But they kept talking.

"You call Vanja cynical, and say her niceness is just an act," Tod said as he squeezed her breasts. "I thought you were her friend."

"I am her friend. I accept her as she is, and she accepts me as I am. We each have qualities the other lacks, and those differences may be useful on occasion." She smiled. "And we both accept you as you are."

"I think I'd better quit while I'm ahead." He paused. "I *am* ahead?"

"Ooh, yes. We both love you." Then she kissed him and squeezed the part inside her, and evoked the culmination. She had evidently been learning things about sex from Vanja, too.

In the morning they breakfasted with Bison, who had supplies to use up lest they be wasted. "Vanja is some creature," he said admiringly. "I was depressed, but she distracted me. A once in a lifetime interaction."

"Once?" Vanja said. "By my count it was six interactions."

The others laughed as Bison colored.

"We should have warned you," Tod said. "She kisses and tells."

"I have not yet begun to tell," Vanja said. "Kissing is the least of it."

"Details are unnecessary," Wizard said sharply.

Vanja glanced at him and was quiet. Tod realized that the old man might be jealous of a performance he could not hope to match. The vampire had misstepped, but probably would not do so again.

They organized, then proceeded along the trail at a rapid pace to reach Bison's terminus. He thanked them all and exited. They watched him enter his house. He would be videophoning Hellene. Would she be as accepting as Vanja had suggested?

Abruptly the trail faded out. They were standing in untracked wilderness.

"She was," Vanja said with satisfaction.

"The avenue for the androids has been closed," Wizard said. "So why isn't our mission over?"

Surprised, Tod checked his internal awareness. The sense of mission remained incomplete. He saw the others reacting similarly.

"What have we overlooked?" Veee asked somewhat plaintively.

Then they saw the rat-sized orange crab. It spied them, saw they were too big to grab, and scuttled back into the brush.

"It's come back to life!" Vanja said, horrified.

"Impossible," Wizard said. "That pool is thoroughly dead."

"Why is the crab so small?" Veee asked.

"A daughter pool!" Bem said.

"It metastasized," Tod said. "We thought we had beaten it, but it was only in remission."

"It what?" Veee asked.

"It is a cancer analogy," Tod said. "A person is seldom killed by the initial tumor. It grows, then metastasizes. That is, it flakes pieces off, which circulate in the blood stream until they find other places to take hold and grow, pretty much randomly. It is one of those daughter tumors that is apt to grow on a vital organ and finally kill the host. As a very general rule, once metastasis occurs, the patient is doomed. Sometimes the parent cell is removed, but it has already metastasized, so it is too late. That's what occurred here: we took out the mother pool, but now there are daughter pools, and we don't know where they are, or how many there are. There may be only one, which we can locate and handle, or hundreds, and the task is hopeless. So our job is not yet done."

"What is remission?"

"Sometimes cancer goes away by itself. But sometimes it only seems to, while the metastasis is occurring. We were foolish not to think of that. Now we're in trouble."

"Unless Wizard can change the communication signal and wipe them all out," Vanja said. "That's why we needed Bison alive: to give us that clue, that we did not value at the time."

"We value it now," Tod said. "He told us how to do radiation treatment."

"Do what?" Veee asked.

"That is when they subject the body to radiation that is bad for all cells, but worse for cancer cells. So the patient is sick, but improving, ironic as that seems. Wizard has to subject the Amoeba to radiation that it may not much like, but it will wipe out the androids. So it's better for the long haul."

Veee turned to Wizard. "Can you do this?"

"I should be able to do it, yes," Wizard said. "But before I can, we must capture a live crab and keep it alive while I test different slants of magic on it. When it collapses, I will know the type of radiation to broadcast. Doing the broadcast will of course exhaust my energy."

"Bem and I will be there for you," Vanja said.

"Which leaves Veee and me to do the dirty work," Tod said. "Catching a live crab."

"Make a net of your poncho," Bem said. "They are small, because the new pool is as yet small."

"Great idea!" Tod took a breath. "Okay, get Wizard rested and ready, while we rustle up a crab."

"They rustle in the foliage?" Veee asked.

"Figure of speech." He thought of something. "Vanja, before you tend to Wizard—"

"I thought you'd never ask." She approached him, flung her arms about him, and kissed him ardently.

"That wasn't what I—"

But she was already transforming and flying away. She had understood, merely done it her way.

"We'll need weapons," Tod said. "Because once we catch one

crab, and the pool realizes what's up, others will attack. They may be small, but we could be overwhelmed by stabbing little horrors if we're not prepared."

They got boots and gauntlets from the villagers, who also promised to set up a halloo if they spied any more crabs. They well understood the danger. Then, armed with knives and clubs they waited for the bat's return.

"I'm glad the mission is not over," Veee said. "Because it means I don't have to think about what happens after it is done."

"We'll say together, one way or another."

"Yes. But Bison's wife left him. That meant their relationship was not perfect despite the marriage. We don't want that to happen to us."

"Good point. We need to iron out any differences we have before it ever comes to that stage."

"If we retire in a village, it will become dull."

"It will never be dull with—"

But she stopped him. "Skip the gallantry. This is serious."

"Maybe Vanja's participation will change it."

"She gets bored faster than we do. I want her with us, and we'll give you all the attention and sex you ever desire. But there has to be something else."

"There has to be something else," he agreed. "Veee, I'm cogitating on it. I admit I like the idea of the constant sexual attention of two women, and want to make it possible. I'll come up with something."

"Do that." It was Vanja, who had come up on them silently from behind and transformed. "I found a pool, not far off. It's little, comparatively, only about a yard across, but it's fully functional. It must have a dozen or so crabs ranging out."

"Show us the way. Then take care of Wizard. He'll need his

strength."

"Follow me." She transformed again and flew high enough so that they could see her over the trees.

The pool turned out to be fairly close, nestled in a swale. Small, yes, but deadly enough. They gazed at it from a distance, assessing its accesses, then went to one of the forming trails.

And there was an orange crab scuttling along. Tod pounced on it, wrapping it in his poncho. It was immediately inert. With luck it had not seen them at all, so the pool would not know what had happened to it. He stuffed the bundle into his knapsack. They walked swiftly down the trail, as it was the way to make the fastest progress.

They were not in luck. Crabs blocked the trail ahead, and then more crabs came up from behind. The pool might be young, but its tactics were inherent in its nature. They would have to fight their way through.

"There are too many of them," Veee said. "They will swarm us and hurt us. They will scramble up your trousers to pierce your legs with their spikes, and up under my skirt. We can't stomp them all."

"Maybe not," Tod said. "The path is narrow here; they have to come at us single file. Of course you've never played golf."

"Golf?"

"It consists of hitting a little ball with a narrow club."

"Tod, these are not balls! They are almost indestructible little monsters."

"Watch me."

Nervously, she watched him.

The first crab charged his foot, its six spiked arms poised for action. It was fearless, being no more than a piece of its pool. Tod swung his club down sideways and caught it in the center, bashing it out of the path and into the brush.

"But it will return," Veee said.

"It will take it a minute or so. Longer if I manage to hit it farther. We can clear them out, then run for it."

She nodded. "I will try your golf."

Tod tackled the downhill crabs and Veee faced back to do the uphill crabs. Their first shots were clumsy, but with practice they got better, until the crabs were being lofted into treetops, thick brush, and briar patches. Veee had the arms for such swings, and was soon striking accurately and forcefully. None of these bashes hurt the androids, but it did take the little monsters increasing time to scramble back into the fray.

They cleared the path for a moment. "Run!" Tod cried as he bashed the last crab into a tangle.

They ran down the path. The crabs soon pursued, but they were now strung out behind, and in any event not as fast on their little feet as the people were.

They reached the village. "Crabs in pursuit!" Tod called. "Stop them!"

The villagers went at it with a will, stabbing at the little legs with knives. The crabs were tough, but not tough enough to withstand the attention of dozens of determined people. Soon they retreated, recalled by the pool.

Tod brought his bundle to Wizard, who was reclining on Bem in lounge form while Vanja massaged his shoulders. "Got one wrapped in the poncho," Tod said.

"Put it in the cage."

Now Tod saw that they had assembled a stout wooden cage with a folding lid. He held the package over the top and let it unwrap, letting the crab drop. He slammed the lid down. "That won't hold it long," Veee warned.

"Be ready to recapture it if it escapes," Wizard said. He stared at the crab as it reanimated and tried to scramble out, balked by the bars.

The crab stabbed at a bar with a spike. The wood cracked. It stabbed with another spike. Indeed, the cage was only a temporary restraint.

Wizard merely sat there, focusing. There was a faint shimmer of magic. That was all.

The third spike splintered the wood. The crab would soon escape. "Better find the range soon," Tod said, readying his poncho.

"I am not finding it," Wizard said. "Rather, I am not able to affect it. It seems to be protected from change."

"Uh-oh," Tod said. "Could be a mutation, or maybe each daughter pool develops its own frequency to distinguish it from the mother pool."

"Trouble," Vanja said. "An orange swarm."

Indeed, an orange layer was flowing across the ground toward them: hundreds of mouse-sized crabs. Tod and the others, including a number of villagers, went out to intercept them with golf clubs, but the cunning creatures avoided the strikes and scuttled on past them.

"The pool has caught on that we're up to something," Bem said. "It may not be smart, but it knows that it can't afford to have one of its minions studied. It is going all-out to destroy Wizard."

"Go wrap Wizard," Tod told it. "Protect him from the crabs to the extent you can." Bem went to do it.

"Bring boiling water," Tod told the villagers. "And fire. We have to keep these things clear of Wizard."

The villagers cooperated, but it was evident that they would not be able to stop the crabs in time. The swarm was rapidly closing on Wizard, who still could not get at the signal.

"There are too many of them," Tod said. "A yard-across pool

should not be able to marshal this many crabs."

"I'll do an aerial survey," Vanja said, and transformed. In moment she was a distant speck in the sky.

The villagers scooped out a hasty trench and poured hot water into it. That balked the crabs for a while, but it was difficult to keep enough hot water in it. Wizard still had not found the wavelength. The situation continued desperate.

Vanja returned. "The daughter pool has discovered the mother pool, and is mining it for protoplasm," she reported. "Crabs are hauling out hunks of jelly. That's a huge source."

"No wonder there are so many crabs," Veee said. "They'll soon be bigger."

"Disaster," Tod agreed. "That will enable the daughter pool to become as potent as the mother pool, in hours. We have to stop it before that happens, or we never will."

They looked at Wizard. He was sweating, literally, but not from heat. He was trying but not succeeding.

Tod knew he had to think of something. He remembered something else Bison had said. "If you can't do it for real, try illusion!" Tod cried as he bashed at myriad mice-crabs. The ones he knocked across the field merely got back on their legs and resumed their charge forward. He felt the pain as they started spiking his ankles. "Like color! Change the crabs' color, so maybe they look wrong even if they're not. Like a false error message. Maybe the pool won't have the wit to clear it."

"Ridiculous," Vanja muttered, dancing in place to avoid the crabs going after her ankles. "Illusion can't stop real magic."

"It can if it fouls up the observer," Tod said. "That is, the pool."

"Pft. We're doomed."

They continued fighting off crabs, taking more injuries. This couldn't last much longer. Once the people fell, the crabs would be all over them, literally, going for more vulnerable targets like eyes and genitalia.

Then, abruptly, the crab in the cage turned blue and stopped moving. Three spokes were imbedded in the splitting wood, with a fourth poised. But the fourth strike did not come. "Got it," Wizard said with satisfaction.

"But will it stop the other crabs?" Veee asked.

"Oh, yes. It is doing so now. They can't receive the signal. Tell the villagers the danger is over."

The swarm around them had turned blue and become inert.

"You're sure?" Tod asked, having trouble crediting so sudden a victory. He had suggested it from desperation rather than belief.

"Yes. As soon as I extend it to the full region." Wizard's eyes glazed as he concentrated, extending his magic. They saw a wave of collapsing blue crabs radiating outward. Then Wizard also collapsed. He had exhausted his strength.

"Tell them," Vanja said, putting her arms around Wizard as Bem curled its edges to make a warm cocoon. She was quick to accept what worked, despite her prior doubt.

"He's depleted," Veee said. "We must let him recover."

Tod and Veee addressed the villagers. "Wizard has changed the signal the pools use to contact the androids, or seemed to change it," he announced. "The crabs will all be dead, and the pools will be helpless. Do what you want with the crabs, when you find them, but stay away from the pools, which will take some time to starve."

The villagers understood. They started ranging out into the forest, looking for dead crabs. The women were collecting them in baskets for disposal.

"You did it," Veee told Tod. "You organized the defense."

"Wizard did it."

"You know what I mean. You took charge and told him how." She caught his hand and kissed it.

But instead of being thrilled, Tod experienced a peculiar letdown, as if something had quietly flowed out of him, leaving him psychically depleted. He realized that it was the presence of the Amoeba in his being. It had let him go.

"I feel so lonely," Veee said. Indeed, she looked lost.

"I am now free to return to my frame," Bem reported unhappily, still wrapped around Wizard to warm him.

"So are we all," Vanja agreed. "The Amoeba has released us."

"I feel like crying," Veee said.

"Cry with me," Vanja said.

Veee hugged her and let her tears flow. Vanja cried too.

"May I join you?" Tod asked.

Both women opened their arms to him. Tod joined them in a three-person hug, shedding his own tears.

"What are we going to do?" Veee asked plaintively.

"We're going to stay here," Tod said as his plan jelled in his mind. "And sign up with the Amoeba for the next mission."

Both women drew back their faces and looked at him.

"There are constant missions," Tod said. "The Amoeba summons people to handle them, selected by their essential qualities as they relate to the specific mission. This requires a break-in period as the people meet each other, form a team, learn what it is they have to accomplish, and figure out how to do it. It's not especially efficient, but it works. Think how much better it would be if there were a more professional team, one already integrated and experienced." He took a breath. "We are going to volunteer to be that team."

"But Bem can't stay," Veee said.

"There will be a replacement, one who has whatever qualities the four of us lack for the next mission, to make the new trail mix whole. It may take a while to reorient, but we'll have a jump start on it."

"Will the Amoeba accept that?" Vanja asked.

"It will have to accept, because we are greasing the skid for it. Much easier to accept our willing service, than to discard us and recruit new people. The Amoeba is essentially a passive entity, taking what is offered. It should accept our guidance in this respect. We can provide it with a brain. It should provide us with adventure. It's best for all parties concerned."

Veee and Vanja smiled together. Then they kissed him, together. That was just the beginning.

The next two days were quiet, as the villagers did find dead blue crabs scattered through the forest, and people of other villages made similar reports. There had been a number of daughter pools, spread throughout the region, but all were now nullified.

Tod, Veee, and Vanja indulged in the luxury of unstressed love and sex. They had been under more tension than they had been conscious of during the mission. It had not depleted them physically, in the manner of Wizard, but they were happy to have the recovery time.

Wizard recovered his strength. He agreed with Tod's plan, having no desire to go home to face the enraged giantess queen. Only then did Bem bid the others farewell and depart. "I wish I could remain with you. But my destiny is in my own frame."

"We understand," Tod said. "If that ever changes, you know we will welcome you back."

They watched Bem depart, knowing it would accomplish its own mission of saving its people from the storms. The girls shed more tears. Then Vanja transformed and perched on Bem. She would see it off, as she could conveniently navigate the steep route back.

Soon she returned. "Bem's gone," she reported. "But Bem's trail did not evaporate."

"Bem can come back!" Veee exclaimed. "If it wants to, some later time. We haven't lost it."

"Just as I was able to return," Wizard said. "Though that was some time later."

"We could be long gone," Tod said. Still, it was reassuring.

But would the Amoeba really embrace their offer? Tod thought it should, but uncertainty remained.

Then he felt the presence. "The Amoeba is back!" he exclaimed. It was a wonderful reawakening.

"We know," Vanja said, her eyes sparkling.

"But who will be our fifth member?" Veee asked.

"And what will be our mission?" Wizard added. "We can be sure it will be no cakewalk."

There was a stir in the village. Something was coming.

"Oh, my," Vanja breathed. "It looks like—"

"A unicorn," Wizard said.

"A male," Veee said.

"Maybe it's a stray," Tod said.

The unicorn walked though the village and approached them. He was a large, sleek, muscular, handsome stallion. The girls gazed at him adoringly. Something about girls and equines.

Then the equine figure vanished. In his place stood a large, sleek, muscular, handsome naked man. "I see that you are the members of the team I am supposed to join," he said. "I am sure we will get along capitally. I am Wetzel." He glanced at Veee and Vanja. "Thank you for your honest appreciation of my physical equine and manly qualities, ladies."

"We didn't speak," Vanja protested faintly.

"Ah, but you did, Vanja. You see, I am telepathic. More precisely, I am a telepathic were-unicorn. We're a rare breed. I presume it was for my ability to read minds that I was summoned here, though I do have other qualities." He looked meaningfully at both women, who both blushed.

Tod was dismayed. He had liked the idea of sharing two women. Now it was clear that would change. What had they gotten into?

Wetzel looked at him. "Perhaps I can answer that too, Tod. There is a concept in my mind that I presume stems from the Amoeba and relates to our mission."

"A concept?" Tod asked numbly. "What is it?"

"Beetle Juice. I am as perplexed by it as you are, but there it is."

"We will surely be finding out soon," Wizard said.

AUTHOR'S NOTE

Sometimes stories or novels come into being because they formulate in the author's mind, come together, and will not be denied. Sometimes they are forced out because the author needs money to survive. *Trail Mix* is neither. In January 2011 my wife and I were discussing prospects, as I had some slack time after wrapping up other projects, and she said I should write a novel or series for original publication on Kindle, to try out that venue directly. She reads many books now on Kindle, enjoying their special convenience while deploring their weird formatting typos. My older novels are getting republished there, and some newer ones, but I had never written directly for it with no try at other publication first.

I pondered, and was intrigued by the notion of a path into adventure. I like paths; they show the way through the wilderness that is life, and lead to each person's destiny. Suppose this ordinary man discovers an extraordinary path? One that leads into wildly different things? I have had paths in my fiction before, but generally as a means rather than an end; once you get where you are going the path is finished. My wife said a path is really too simple; what was needed was a trail. A path may lead from your yard to your neighbor's yard, while a trail can cross a continent. Okay, a trail, one on which different people or creatures from drastically different realms can meet, interact, travel, and live. Then it came to me: trail mix. There was my series title.

But who or what made this remarkable trail? And for what purpose? How could it reach across space, time, and alternate realities? Trails generally don't make themselves; they are made. There had to be a reason, a larger purpose. I did not have to explore it far before I came upon the Amoeba, an entity as large as imagination, yet not an active player the way conscious living creatures are. All it knows is that there is a need, and it acts to fill that need, somewhat the way water needs to seek the lowest level. When the need changes, so does the mix, to enable the new job to be done.

And so it may have been with me. There was a need to explore a new venue, and the Amoeba obligingly filled that need. Where the trail will lead, ultimately, who knows? I can see ahead just far enough to know that the next setting is Beetle Juice, otherwise known as the vicinity of the giant red star Betelgeuse, where there are beetles galore. You have not seen beetles like these; Earth is a beetle backwater. But why would a telepathic were-unicorn be needed to deal with mere beetles? Could that be overkill, or is there some less obvious trait he has that fills the need? Stay tuned.

Writers are urged to write what they know. This becomes difficult in fantasy, which is the literature of the impossible. But for verisimilitude—that means the semblance of truth—some homey details help. One example is the ocarina, which is a real musical instrument as described in the novel, modeled on the one my daughter gave me. I can't play it nearly as well as Tod does, but it has a lovely flute-like, or more properly recorder-like sound regardless. Another is Tod's knife, which I bought years ago, just in case, a deadly double-sided blade labeled *Fury*, illegal in some regions. I'm not a knife fighter, I merely want a way to defend myself if I ever have to. In close quarters a knife is said to be as lethal as a gun. I hope I never have to put that to the test. My experience with guns is limited to my training in the US Army more than fifty years ago; I was a good shot then, and retain respect for what a gun can do. Another is the forest. I lived for years in a house in the forest as a child, and as an adult I now live on a small tree farm I own. So I am familiar with forestland, and with blueberry glades, and love them. Though not with the alien trees and berries along the Amoeba trail.

I also made the characters ordinary in their assorted fashions, even Bem, whom you would surely like in person, and Vanja, who may be a true vampire but would heat the bed of any normal male. That's so readers can identify with them, and see things from their viewpoints. But no, I can't say I know anyone quite like her; she's not drawn from life. Otherwise my wife would never understand.

One note of appreciation: for Rudy Reyes, who proofread the manuscript, catching a number of errors I had missed.

Readers interested in learning more of me and my works can visit my www.hipiers.com web site, where I have a monthly column, information about my works, and an ongoing survey of electronic publishers, or my new blog site, piersanthonyblog.blogspot.com.